T0247446

Also by Marianne K. Martin

Legacy of Love
Love in the Balance
Dawn of the Dance
Never Ending
Mirrors
Under the Witness Tree
Dance in the Key of Love
For Now, For Always

Mirrors

Marianne K. Martin

Ann Arbor

Bywater Books, Inc.
PO Box 3671
Ann Arbor MI 48106-3671

Printed in the United States of Amerrica on acid-free paper

Bywater Books First Edition: July 2010

This book was first published by Bella Books, Inc., in August 2001 and had a second printing in January 2003.

Cover design: Bonnie Liss (Phoenix Graphics)

ISBN 978-1-932859-72-0

Mixed Sources
Product group from well-managed
forests and other controlled sources
www.fsc.org Cert no. SW-COC-002283
© 1996 Forest Stewardship Council

For Jo

Acknowledgments

The author would like to acknowledge and thank the following people:

Kelly Smith, for her vision and development of Bywater Books, and for her commitment to the advancement of our literature.

Lila Empson, whose sharp eye and diligence in the editing process is much appreciated.

Delishia White and Zakiyah Thomas-White, for their time given in proofreading and for sharing with me an intimate look into the black lesbian community.

Gloria Root, for her perspective and confirmations as a high school counselor and for the time taken to proofread.

Ilene Johnson, for her proofreading time and her expertise as a high school teacher.

Terri and Jane, for patience and time taken from their P-town vacation to add their personal experiences to the author's understanding.

My best friend and partner, Jo, for her immeasurable support and love.

One

The perimeter of the bedroom, like the rest of Shayna Bradley's house, was an entry straight out of a Showcase of Homes tour. Professionally draped window treatments, "socks-only" carpet, eucalyptus and silk-flower arrangements. Testimony to an organized life and a disciplined mind.

The center of the room, however, resembled the aftermath of a tornado touchdown. Shoes and clothes and pillows were strewn about the floor. A moat of pink-and-purple bedspread circled the foot of the bed; splayed on the bed's surface was a tangle of satin brown arms and legs wrapped in slips of a stark white sheet.

Shayna stirred in sleepy-morning consciousness and stretched her arm over the curve of Serena's back. Baby-smooth skin was cooled now of last night's passion. The breath that had whispered its searing messages against Shayna's neck now breathed evenly across her abdomen, and broke gently into a moan.

"No, baby," Serena said softly. "Don't go gettin' up yet." Shayna smiled to herself, made a conscious effort to reset her internal clock, and asked, "What do you have in mind?"

Serena stretched into a groan and resettled into the same position. "Can't you manage one day without a schedule? Weekends—" she stretched her hand up to Shayna's shoulder and caressed down over the sculptured biceps "—are mine. Remember?"

"That's not what I meant." At least not what I want you to think I meant. Exasperating, this business of love affairs. How are they supposed to fit congenially into daily dealings with devastated lives and uncertain futures? How much comparative time do they deserve next to saving threatened careers and lost child-custody?

"Yes, it is," Serena was saying. "Those words coming from someone else might be tellin' me what I'm wantin' to hear. But from you they mean 'Maybe one more go at it, then I'm outta this bed.'"

Shayna laughed a soft husky tone that admitted only a smidgen of guilt for the truth in Serena's words. "So," Shayna smiled, "one more go at it?"

"Uh-huh, but how am I gonna know whether saying no would punish you or me?"

A playful raise of Shayna's eyebrows hinted that it would be more Serena's loss, but the ring of the telephone stifled any response.

"Don't," Serena warned with a shake of her head. Shayna dropped her head back onto the pillow and closed her eyes. The phone rang again. Her struggle was obvious. She lifted her head and stole a look at the caller-ID screen. Her eyes never returned to Serena. A forceful slap stung her thigh as she reached for the phone.

Jean's voice was light and airy and unmistakable. "Are you busy?"

"Hm, let's see. It's Sunday morning. Serena just crawled out of my bed. Nope, I guess not."

"Oh, I'm sorry. Apologize for me and give me a call later, okay?"

"No. Showering together is really counterproductive, and it'll be another thirty minutes before I can grab the last of the hot water." Shayna laughed softly. "I'm going to either have to get another girlfriend or a bigger hot-water heater." She stretched fully onto her back. "Talk to me."

"It's probably nothing."

"It is something if it's bothering you. What is it?"

"Just a feeling. Something doesn't feel right at school."

Shayna's little coaxing was all that was needed. "We have a new teacher this year, and I think he's gay."

"Are you worried that he's too obvious?"

"No. He's not at all. Something caught my attention—I'm not even aware of what it was—and I found myself looking more closely. I noticed things like his eyes not wandering over women when they weren't looking. But I didn't see him looking at men either, so I dismissed it. I also noticed that he didn't show even mild interest in either of the attractive female student teachers, but I thought he could be committed to a girlfriend. Something, though, made me keep watching him. It's as if he's too careful, too within the lines. I don't know how to explain it. Anyway, no one has said anything about him. In fact, no one has said anything about him being out of school for a week, either. And that is weird."

"What would be normal?"

"For the teachers in adjacent rooms, or someone he eats lunch with, to tell others what's going on. Someone always knows whether it's illness or a family death or whatever. This time, though, we all got an administrative memo telling us to explain to students that he is ill."

"He's new, Jean, he may not be close enough with anyone yet. Or if he is gay, maybe he's just staying private on purpose."

"I hope that's all it is."

"Could you be reading more into this because of what happened to Katherine? Seeing firsthand the unfairness and the pressure that a lesbian teacher can face is about as close to it as you could get without it actually happening to you. Maybe that's causing you to anticipate a problem where there isn't one."

"Maybe you're right. It's not like I don't have anything else to worry about. I guess I should concentrate on my own business. I'm hardly ready for the discussion with Ken that I feel coming. He's made reservations at my favorite restaurant for tomorrow night."

"Monday night? Football night?"

"Uh-huh. A night so sacred that school-board meetings were set for the first Tuesday of each month."

3

"So maybe he's just trying to show you how much he loves you."

"Maybe. Speaking of relationships, though, I think I've kept you on the phone too long already. I'd better let you go before Serena starts to hate me. Apologize for me?"

"No problem."

Two

An emergency faculty meeting almost always meant one thing—something bad had happened, either to one of the students or to one of the faculty. Usually someone always knew what and who, and by the time they were seated so did most of the staff.

Today's meeting, however, held the mystique of government espionage. Absent were the whispered rumors filtering through the returning faculty. There had been no hint, no word. The reason for this meeting would be a surprise to all but one.

Jean Kesh took a seat at a large round table in the middle of a library filled with questioning frowns and blank stares. The smell of shop dust and motor oil and a whisper over her left shoulder greeted her immediately.

"If the Admiral doesn't show up in the next five minutes, let's you and me take an early lunch at the Holiday Inn." Brian Wilkens dropped a massive set of keys noisily onto the table and plopped himself into the chair next to Jean.

"And if he does show up," she returned matter-of-factly, "why don't I just give Ken a call and tell him to fix his own dinner tonight?" She grinned. *Fat chance, even if you shook the flakes of sawdust from that mat of salt-and-pepper curls ... even if I did have the courage for divorce.* "What's this meeting all about?"

If anyone on the staff had any prior warning, it would be Brian. He had paved his own private path to the main office with his military tales, sports wagers, and an innate understanding of the mechanics of the inner circle.

"It's not one of the kids, or I would've known by now—must be faculty."

And too serious even for Brian to know.

A second later, their attention centered on Chad Ellerton, entering the room like the upright cousin of a grizzly and with the presence of a boot-camp sergeant. Fresh from military retirement, he was a well-intentioned school board's answer to better school discipline. A principal with by-the-letter demands and people skills that could barely coax a D from a 130 IQ.

"This will be a short meeting," he began. "What I have to say won't take long, and there shouldn't be any need for discussion. Lunch period has been lengthened, and fifth period shortened by fifteen minutes."

Jean easily interpreted Brian's groan. His fifth-period wood shop would not have the time needed to set up, get any amount of work done, and clean up by the end of the period. They would end up in the dreaded classroom with whatever impromptu assignment Brian could come up with. Her fifth period class, on the other hand, would be thrilled with dance music and Ping-Pong and not having to change clothes.

The Admiral was fussing uncharacteristically with a folder he carried. "This is a touchy subject," he explained. "I didn't want memos lying around for students to find."

The room buzzed while he hesitated to remember which wording he had decided on. The buzzing stopped when he cleared his throat.

"Come on, man," Brian blurted. "What's going on?"

"I'm getting to it," he said, adding a twitch of a smile to the pink flush of his cheeks. "The short of it is, Dan Sanders won't be coming back." The hush held. "We told everyone that he's been sick for the past week in order to give the school board time to

6

meet. The student body will be told that he had to leave due to health reasons."

Brian again. "So what's the real reason?"

The Admiral chuckled nervously. "Well, let's just say that we would've been monitoring one of the locker rooms ... and it wouldn't have been Jean's."

Jean shook her head. "He handles things so professionally," she muttered, then raised her voice. "What's the problem? Is he gay? A pedophile?"

"Queer as a three-dollar bill."

Such a progressive mind.

"I flushed guys like that out of my command without asking and without telling."

Brian turned in his chair to face Jean. "Yeah, I served with a guy like that," he said with a low voice. "And under fire he would've pulled Admiral Asshole's big white butt into a bunker before I would've."

Meanwhile, the offhanded information computed into a whir of questions that circled and jumped from table to table.

"What did he do? Did he say something inappropriate in a class or something?"

Ellerton, with another clearing of his throat, said, "Well, we're lucky there. We got him out of here before anything did happen."

"But he is making history fun for the kids. They love him."

Brian spoke up quickly. "So you yank out a perfectly good tooth because it might someday have a cavity? You can't fire someone as a preventative."

"Yes, they can," Jean offered quietly. "And not just here at the high-school level." They can make assumptions based on rumor, force you to admit or deny, and make your professional life a miserable mess regardless of how good a teacher you are. Her thoughts were never far from her friend Katherine and what she had been through at the university. And she knew that being blond and feminine and soft-spoken wasn't her own saving grace.

In physical education, being married was the only thing that kept her from watching her own back.

"Doesn't the union give him any protection?" Brian was asking.

Jean shook her head. "There's no protection against immorality. Being gay is immoral in this state."

Loud enough for everyone's ears, Brian said, "He can sleep with a cocker spaniel for all I care. We should be concerned about losing a damn good teacher."

White, middle class, male. Drinks beer regularly, watches football religiously, loves his muscle car, and although married for twenty-odd years has an unhealthy need to flirt with good-looking women. Jean smiled to herself. As unlikely a champion of gay rights as one would ever find, and definitely his most redeeming quality.

"Save your breath, Brian," she advised. "And don't burn your membership card to the inner circle. It's not going to make any difference."

Student adviser Edwards uncrossed his arms and shifted around in his chair. "So, Brian, if he slept with cocker spaniels would you leave him in charge of the kennel?"

"See?" Jean muttered. But, for her own peace of mind, she would be making a call to the one person who would know for sure if Dan Sanders had any chance at all in court.

Three

"I was right." Jean's voice on the other end of the phone was clearly agitated. "They fired Dan Sanders today."

Shayna's voice remained its usual calm. "The one you thought was gay."

"Yes."

"For being gay?"

"Yes. I guess he didn't, or couldn't, deny it."

"Because if it were for any other reason he'd have a fighting chance."

Jean sighed. "Sadly, that answers my question. I was hoping the new legislation would offer some protection."

"For students." Shayna said. "If they're willing to go to court over it. But not for teachers. Not in Michigan or thirty-nine other states. Nothing's changed since Gerry Crane was 'encouraged' to resign from Byron Center. He could try to fight it, but unless your school district has specific wording in the contract that protects him, Mr. Sanders would be wasting his time and money."

"This makes me angry all over again. It's taken me three years to believe that Katherine's okay after having to leave the university. Now this."

"Is he a good teacher?"

"Excellent. Fresh, funny, interesting—the kids love him."

"I'm sorry."

"Yes, I am too."

After a momentary silence, Shayna coaxed, "Tell me something good."

Jean's voice gained an upward lilt. "You know you should be in the psychology field."

"Mostly common sense. Come on, what do you have?"

"They're giving me a chance to convince the school board to keep the Life Fit classes in the curriculum."

"There you go."

"It's only a chance, probably a thin one."

"Is that a half-empty glass you have sitting in front of you again?"

Jean couldn't contain a much-needed chuckle. "No, now that I look more closely, it's actually half full. And you're practicing without a license." She listened to Shayna's familiar laugh and felt her spirit lighten even more.

"Coming to the gym after work tomorrow?"

"Why is it that I can't convince you that I get enough exercise teaching five PE classes a day?"

"It's not the same kind of exercise. Besides, you keep me honest."

"And I could use the adult socialization."

Shayna replied quickly. "I didn't say that."

"I thought I'd beat you to it. I'll see you tomorrow."

Four

"You've hardly touched your dinner," Ken managed between the last forkfuls of mashed potatoes. "Are you sure you're feeling all right?"

Jean absently pushed her applesauce into a neat line with the edge of her fork. "I guess I'm not very hungry."

"You've been so quiet I feel as if I've been talking to myself all evening."

"I've had a lot on my mind," she said with a faint smile.

"This Dan Sanders thing is still bothering me, and there's the presentation to the school board. I've been listening, though."

"So it isn't that the company is boring?" He offered her his little-boy grin and a wink. "Well, I'm not going to insult you by ordering dessert when there's half a homemade German chocolate cake waiting at home." He rose and fished his wallet from the breast pocket of his favorite black suit. "I'll get the bill and we'll get out of here."

Jean wasn't fooled. She knew he recognized this mood and was trying not to let it bother him. It wasn't only what was going on at school. They had talked about that. She brought too much of the day home with her each night, but that wasn't what was distancing her tonight. It was what they hadn't talked about in a long time, and tonight's mood was an indication of a decision she suspected he wasn't ready to hear.

Ken, with the kind of patience that could qualify him for sainthood, had been true to his promise for a full year now. He hadn't mentioned having children even once, hadn't discussed transforming the basement into a children's playroom, hadn't brought up the college fund. No pressure, just as she had asked. In return, she had promised not to speak of separation. Pressure-free normalcy, or as near to it as they could get.

Yet there had been pressure, building noticeably over the past couple of months, raising Jean's anxiety level and making her irritable. And it came, she finally realized, from within herself. All the times she had scrutinized his every word, waiting for a chastizable inflection in his voice, and all the times she had hoped he would argue or yell or give her any viable excuse— all those times she should have scrutinized herself and demanded confrontation.

Jean felt an affectionate squeeze of her hand as Ken brought the car to a crunching stop in the gravel drive of their west-side home. The trip from the restaurant had been a silent one, with nothing to interrupt her thoughts until they were in their own living room.

Ken pulled her to him, kissed her gently on the lips, then tilted his head to look into her eyes. She returned his gaze with the subtlety of a smile that was meant to tell him she still wasn't ready to talk.

If she had been after looks, she thought, she couldn't have done a whole lot better. Even at forty, there were only fine crow's-feet lines violating the pink smoothness of his cheeks. His blue eyes still held the sparkle of innocence. And if she had been after personality, she had hit the jackpot. He was kind and thoughtful and faithful. She had chosen well. He had been her best friend for years, and that was what made her decision nearly impossible.

"Gonna have some cake with me?" he asked.

"Sure," she replied with a kiss to his cheek. "I'll get it."

℞ ℞ ℞

12

"Your mom mentioned that you two had a long talk the other day," Ken began, placing his empty plate on the coffee table.

Jean left the last bite of cake on her plate and stacked it on top of his. "Uh-huh." *So it begins, unless I delay once more a discussion that cannot be avoided forever.* "She doesn't understand why I won't take a year off school to have a baby. She's sure that I'm wasting the best years of my life on other people's children."

"And you know I agree with her."

Her tone became decidedly defensive. "I touch a lot more children's lives by teaching."

"Nobody is asking you to stop teaching, just to take some time off."

"Then go back to work for a year or two, and then take another year off for another child. Each time it means a permanent substitute at school and complete disruption of my programs. That kind of disruption wreaks havoc with discipline, and it could even mean elimination of parts of my program, like Life Fit."

"It's done all the time. It seems like a minimal sacrifice to make for your own family." Ken hunched forward, elbows heavily on his thighs, his focus on his hands hanging limply between his knees. "The school will adapt, the kids will adapt. It happens every year in every school system." He looked up to find Jean's eyes on his. "Are you afraid you won't be able to adapt?"

She forced herself not to look away. "Maybe."

His eyes dropped their focus. She was widening the break in his heart, but there was no way to stop it now. A fine, hairline crack had formed years ago when she had chosen her career over children. Each rejection by Jean in the bedroom, each demand for contraception, had worked to widen the break. Open-ended discussions had held out temporary hope, but each year the voice of time had spoken louder and healing had become less likely.

Ken's voice was soft, the expression on his face miraculously hopeful. "I still think once you had a baby and heard it cry and held it to your breast, your maternal instincts would be so strong that there would be no doubt that you had made the right decision."

13

Then he spoke the words that had always before bought him time. "You would be such a good mother. We would have the luckiest child in the world."

But not this time. She couldn't do this to him any longer. "I don't understand why I feel the way I do, Ken. All I know is that it wouldn't be right to bring a child into this world while I'm so unsure. I've seen too many kids at school whose parents should have had this discussion. Kids who should have had a stay-at-home parent when they were young."

"Honey, that wouldn't be us. We—"

"No." Jean cupped the warmth of his cheek. "I didn't mean to hurt you like this. I don't know how to tell you I'm sorry, except by not doing this to you any more."

"Don't do this," he pleaded. "I can make that sacrifice. I will make it. Just let me."

"I've been selfish. I thought because I loved you that it was all right. But I just continue hurting you."

He took her hands. "No, Jean. If—"

"Which hurt is worse?" she continued. "The one that keeps you from being the father you have every right to be, or the one that comes from us ending a marriage and trying to remain friends?"

"I can't imagine making a life with anyone else." He pulled her into an embrace as tears filled his eyes. "I don't want anyone else. I can sacrifice not having children."

"Maybe," she said, losing the fight to keep her own tears at bay. "But you wouldn't be happy. Maybe you've already begun to resent me. I can't stand the thought that you resent me."

Ken straightened out of their embrace. "I don't. Please believe me, I don't. I love you. We can work through this," he said. He lifted her face with his hand and looked into tear-filled eyes. "Tell me you're not going to give up on us."

The tears now coursed over Jean's cheeks. She closed her eyes, unable to face his hopefulness, unable to admit her fear. "I can't stay here," she said as she stood.

He reached for her arm as she turned away, but Jean pulled free. "Jean, don't leave. Please don't leave."

"I just can't be here tonight." She tried to hurry toward the door, surprised at the weakness of her legs. Her thoughts had become carefully spoken over time, but not until now had they come to action. Her resolve was nearly as shaky as her legs.

Just for tonight. Maybe not to have to see his tears. God, the hurt in his eyes. Just a night or two away, she promised herself. Or maybe just tonight.

She continued straight ahead, out the door, down the steps, wiping the tears from her face and not looking back. If she looked back, she would see him watching from the porch, feel him pulling her, wanting her, and she would turn around. She would hold him and console him and tell him that she did love him, and nothing would be resolved.

By rote, the Camry reached the end of their block and turned toward the highway. She had resisted looking in the rearview mirror and now picked up speed to widen the distance that would strengthen her determination.

Fifteen minutes later, Jean pulled to the back of her parents' driveway, turned off the key, and rested her head against the top of the steering wheel. The shaking now began at the base of her spine and reverberated to the ends of her fingers and toes.

She wasn't sure how long she sat there before she saw a flood of light and heard her father's voice. "Jean? Jean, what's wrong?"

What am I doing? Here of all places. What's wrong with my mind? I should be at Moni's or Shayna's, or a motel, for God's sake. But it was too late to do anything else. She emerged from the car and met the comfort of her father's and then her mother's arms.

"It's so late, honey. Is everything all right?" There was obvious concern in Ernie Carson's voice.

Before she could answer, Mary Carson voiced her own concern. "Is Ken okay?"

"Yes and yes," Jean replied. "I didn't mean to alarm you. I just need some time to myself." She added with a kiss to her mother's cheek, "And no more questions. At least until tomorrow."

Ernie snapped off the yard light and relocked the back door. Just as he had all of her life, he would attend to the practical matters at hand, return to his late night program, and catch up on anything else over morning coffee. Her father only needed to know that his daughter was in his home and safe.

Mary, on the other hand, was already bustling about the kitchen. "I'll get you a nice cup of chamomile tea. It'll calm you so you can sleep. Come and sit in the kitchen with me and we'll talk about whatever it is."

"No, Mom." She would flutter on all night if Jean let her. There would be praises for Ken, good parent material, faithful, high moral fiber; there would be reasons upon reasons for staying with him forever. And there would be no allowance for any decision to the contrary. "I need to be by myself. Please try to understand," she said with a step backward and a hopeful little curl at the corners of her mouth. She said good night and made her way down the hall and up the stairs to the room she had occupied for so many of her younger years.

Maybe she would talk with them tomorrow. Then again, maybe there was nothing to talk about.

Five

Rising way before her retired folks had any need to meet the day, and leaving for work an hour before necessary, was clearly avoiding the issue, but it was the best Jean felt she could do today.

Her court shoes squeaked noticeably on the freshly polished surface as she strode the length of the empty hallway. The air carried only a hint of the hundreds of teenaged bodies that would soon be coursing noisily through the halls. This was the cleanest she had seen the building maintained in the ten years she'd been teaching here. Cleanliness was the most apparent by-product of the Admiral's military training, and it was the only one she could think to be grateful for at the moment.

She continued past the auto shop where Brian was undoubtedly under the lift, changing the oil in the Ram, a two-thousand-mile ritual he practiced as faithfully as her mother attended Sunday mass. Although their friendship had allowed discussions as personal as the death of Brian's father, she wasn't willing to encourage another invitation to run away and make mad passionate love with him on a sandy beach somewhere in the Bahamas. She'd take her chance on getting through the day without telling anyone that her personal life was beginning a painful metamorphosis. A day filled with five hundred plus teenagers has a way of commanding one's full attention. Personal pain would be competing with boisterous boys, flirting girls, and the beginning of a new and traditionally unpopular physical education unit.

By third period, the anesthetization was in full effect. The groan rumbling through the gym was universally male, as were the protests.

"No way. I'm not comin' to class."

"You're crazy. That's a girls' game!"

"You can't make us play a girls' game."

The protests weren't new, they weren't even original. Jean had heard them all before, and over the years she had developed her own approach to handling them.

"First of all, badminton requires the quickest reactions of any court game. The shuttlecock—" she ignored the snickers and their implications "—when hit correctly can travel a short distance at a speed of seventy miles an hour."

She endured the expressions of disbelief and continued. "The video you will be seeing in a few minutes is last year's men's national championship doubles match. I think you will be surprised. Second—" she looked directly at Jay Markus, five-foot-eleven, and always a half grade point away from basketball ineligibility "—anyone who can beat me once during the next six weeks will receive an automatic A for the semester."

Shouts of bravado and more disbelief were mixed with the expected questions. "Yes, even if you've skipped every other day of class," Jean replied, "and you show up for one day and are lucky enough to beat me, you've got the A." She smiled and pulled the video cart into position. "Of course, if you lose …"

The first day away from Ken couldn't have happened at a better time. It was the first Tuesday of the month and, from the moment she had crawled out of bed that morning until she would collapse back into it again after the school-board meeting tonight, she would have little time to reflect on her personal life. For that, Jean was grateful.

However, in the only moments of calm that she'd had all day

18

her resolve not to confide in anyone began to slip. She looked over at Shayna, straining through the final repetitions of her hamstring curls. Perspiration glistened across the darkness of her brow; veins pulsed predominately from her temple and her neck. No high-school boys would dare brag their macho prowess and accuse her of lifting Q-tips.

Despite Shayna's claim, no one needed to be with her to keep her honest, especially one as uncommitted to lifting weights as Jean. Shayna's body had been developed long before Jean had come into the picture and had been maintained throughout a three-year friendship, regardless of how many times Jean had actually shown up to work out.

Honesty ran like a golden thread through the fabric of Shayna Bradley's life—a strong, glittering continuum obvious in everything from her workouts to her career to her friendships. Getting an honest opinion from her would be a given.

The words escaped before a second thought. "I'm staying at my parent's house." I'm starting a new life.

Shayna looked up immediately, surprise registering in the light brown eyes. "Wanna talk about it?"

But she wasn't ready for opinions yet. "No." Although she might be able to say the word separation in her head, she wasn't ready to say it out loud, not even to Shayna.

Shayna rose from the bench. "Okay," she said, bending from the waist and sliding her hands down the back of her legs to gradually stretch the tight hamstrings. "Do you have time to grab something to eat?"

"I have the school board presentation tonight to prepare for. I can't take the time. I'm feeling a tremendous amount of pressure to save the Life Fit program, and I don't think it's even possible."

"Ah, Jean of little faith," she said shaking her head. "I looked over the notes you gave me. They're very thorough, very convincing. Besides—" Shayna pulled the neck of her T-shirt up to wipe the sweat from her face "—it's well known how important fitness is and how unfit our youth are."

"Yes, but this program is designed specifically for those kids who traditionally fail regular physical education classes—overweight kids, asthmatics, any kid who, by putting them in a regular class, we'd be setting up for ridicule and failure." Jean picked up her water bottle, but continued with hardly a pause. "It is the kind of program that gets tossed on the scrap pile when a bond election fails. I'm facing an impossible task. We're supposed to be responsible for educating all students, not just the easy ones. But I don't know if I can make someone else feel the same kind of responsibility that I feel for these kids."

"Didn't you tell me one of them died last year?"

Jean nodded. "Not a student at the time. She'd been out of school for four years, trying to make a life for herself at three hundred-plus pounds. She had a heart attack, as young as she was. She'd been excused from physical education every single year for one excuse or another. We failed her."

"You're right, it is everyone's responsibility, and that includes parents and doctors. So don't be so tough on yourself; she was an extreme case."

"Extreme are the statistics. There's all this attention on breast cancer now, but that only accounts for one death in twenty-seven. One of every two women will die from either heart attack or stroke, and that is something we know we can do something about. This program helps keep those kids who are most at risk from being embarrassed or intimidated into failure."

Shayna raised her eyebrows and smiled. "Pretty passionate presentation right there. Why do you doubt yourself? You did all your homework; you have all the facts."

She'd come to expect this feeling, crisp and clear as a breath of pure oxygen. When she was with Shayna, her mind was focused and sure and, for at least a brief time, free of self-doubt. The feeling was so addictive that Jean found herself making every effort to extend the time she spent with Shayna. Selfish in some respects, but Shayna didn't seem to mind.

"What are you worried about?" Shayna asked.

"That maybe this is too important to me. That all that passion may look like frustration or fanaticism. It took a lot of trust for those kids to give this program and me a chance. I'm worried that I'll let them down."

"Okay, get your stuff and make that a quick shower. We'll go to the coffee shop and get a sandwich while I find out how many middle-aged, out-of-shape businessmen are holed up in this head of mine. I'll ask the questions and argue the points like a board member totally out-of-touch with the state of our youth and whose bottom line is how many dollars he can divert into the next conference trip. How's that?"

Jean smiled in amazement. "So you've been to our school board meetings."

"Close enough. Come on, I've only got two hours to turn you into a lawyer."

Six

The answering machine was flashing an eerie red glow over the darkened room. Shayna dropped her briefcase next to the couch and hit the message button.

"Okay, you're running late and forgot to call again."

Serena's voice had a tone that would probably hide the irritation from anyone but Shayna. "I'm on my way over to Tanita's. I don't want them holdin' up the eats for us."

"Shit," Shayna snapped as the second message followed quickly on the heels of the first.

"Why do you even have a cell phone if you're not going to use it? Everyone is asking where you are. I've made the last excuse I'm going to make for you."

Shayna checked her watch, gratefully listening to her brother's message reminding her of her parents' anniversary party as she tried to decide between a call to Tanita's or a very late arrival.

Serena decided for her with her third message. "If you don't show up tonight, don't bother to call me again."

An unintentional lapse in memory. She had just forgotten—again. Not every time had involved a gathering at Tanita's, but too many of her lapses had involved Serena's friends. And there had been too many other excuses, no matter how valid they were in Shayna's mind. The point of the impending argument was predictable.

Music pounded its beat from uncounted speakers as Shayna offered her apologies and made her way through the large group of mostly black, mostly heterosexual, men and women spilling into every room of the main floor of Tanita and Bobby's house. She smiled cordially, listened politely to sports predictions that held no interest for her, and stealthily avoided a political argument that centered on the Republican courtship of the black vote.

"What's up, Shayna?" Tanita greeted as she brushed by with the necks of three beer bottles pinched between the fingers of each hand. "Serena's in the kitchen with Billy and them. While you're in there, make yourself a plate of food before it's gone."

Shayna squeezed around the corner of the kitchen and heard Serena before she saw her.

"Yeah, and if we keep working for their companies," Serena emphasized, "we're not going to get the promotions and we're only making them richer."

"That's changing," a young black man countered from across the table. "If you look hard enough, there are advancement opportunities out there. Besides, there aren't enough black-owned businesses to employ us for what we're worth. How many of us does your uncle's real estate company carry? Mostly family, right? What would you have us do?"

Shayna slid behind Serena's chair and acknowledged the young black man with a smile.

Serena continued without a pause. "We need to stop supporting white corporate America with our talents and our money—"

"You can't target big corporations," he insisted. "There are too many jobs involved. Boycotting jobs plays right into their hands. We should be fighting to keep affirmative action."

"We have to make sacrifices to start our own companies. More of us have to take the risk to be independent, like Shayna." It was the first indication Serena had made that she knew Shayna was standing behind her. "Eventually, she'll pull in big money as an independent attorney."

"I share office expenses with a white man," Shayna clarified. "Effective change has to occur from within the system. And black businesses have to widen their market; they can't survive solely on black money. It's a slow process."

"Way too slow for me," added the dark-skinned woman to Serena's left. "Affirmative action doesn't go far enough. Three years, and I'm still sitting at the same desk."

Forgotten elements of the quotient, Shayna thought. Ambition, drive, education. An invalid argument based on inaccurate and insufficient data. She hated listening to it and not rebutting. But she knew from past conversations to keep her thoughts on this topic to herself, unless she was ready to incite a heated argument here as well as a private one later tonight. Discrimination and injustice constituted a huge war. She personally preferred battles that could be won in the near future, ones closer to home for a black lesbian. Besides, there was already one inevitable battle facing her tonight.

"Coming over?" Shayna asked.

They stood at the end of an uncomfortable silence beside the bright red mustang, the payments for which kept Serena living with her sister and three kids. The October nights now required a minimum of a sweater, and even then challenged one to stand for long without shivering.

Yet the arms folded across Serena's chest acted more to bolster her defense than to provide warmth. She stared over the hood of the car as a flash of light from the opening door illuminated the sidewalk and a few friends as they left the house.

Shayna's attention remained on Serena's face and the expression that was becoming far too familiar. She was still standing there, Shayna decided, because there were so many things that she loved about this woman. A long list, now that she thought about it—Serena's pride and her loyalty; the delicious curl of her full upper lip as it widened into a brilliant smile; the care she took each month to perm shoulder-length hair and curl it into soft, shiny curls; the mischievous gleam that shows in her eyes at the beginning of foreplay; and the feel of her skin, satin-smooth and heated with passion.

Other things, however, strained her tolerance. At the top of that list was an annoying attitude of racial exclusiveness—a direct slap, however unintentional, in the face of Shayna's white mother.

Serena's breath showed visibly in a smoky vapor as she spoke. "What was so important this time?"

"It wasn't that it was so important, it was that I just forgot."

"You forgot because something else was more important to you." The threat in her eyes promised that her anger was about to escalate. "Don't make me guess."

Shayna relented. "Jean—"

Serena threw open her arms and spun on her heels to turn her back to Shayna.

"She needed help for a school-board presentation she had to give tonight. Don't blame her; she didn't ask for the help. I'm sorry, Serena, I just forgot."

"Wrong direction," she said, whirling back to face Shayna.

"I don't blame Jean. I may not like her, but I don't blame her. You, though ..." She planted her hands severely on her hips. "Why is it that we're still together?" She moved her head from side to side.

Shayna cringed at the motion and Serena's obvious attempt to irritate her.

"Because we kick it so good?"

"This is about Jean." Shayna nodded her head for emphasis. "It's about enjoying her friendship. It's about working out, and classical music, and learning to play tennis ... it's about being too white."

"Why do you do those things, Shayna? To foster your African heritage?"

Shayna snapped her arms up in front of her. "Look at these wrists," she demanded. "See any shackles on them?" She pointed at her feet. "How about these ankles? See any chains? No. You're damn right you don't. I'm a free woman. Been free all my life. Free to be whoever and whatever I choose." She started to turn away but stopped. "No one is going to put ancient chains on me, least of all you. If you can't accept me for who I am, we haven't a snowball's chance in hell of taking this relationship any further than it is right now."

She nearly completed her turn this time, but Serena grabbed her arm. "Don't play counselor with me, spoutin' off and walkin' away." She swung Shayna's arm back forcefully and stepped squarely in front of her. "You don't intimidate me."

"I'm not trying to."

"I'm not afraid to argue with you. Why don't we get it all out there, huh? All the ugly truth." Serena moved her head from side to side again, pushing the edges of Shayna's tolerance. "You want to talk truth, right? The truth is, you don't want this relationship goin' any further. It's been over a year, and I'm still just spendin' the night. Think that's not tellin' me something?"

"Keep your voice down," Shayna warned. "Your friends are going to know that you're having an argument with your girlfriend. Such good friends that you aren't even out to them. Besides—" she made a decisive turn toward the car "—you do not want to go toe to toe with me."

Serena shouted after her as Shayna crossed the middle of the street. "Or anything to anything with you again." She raised her voice even louder. "At least my friends know where they came from."

The traffic lights through town blinked red, and traffic was sparse. Shayna traveled the familiar streets and stopped routinely at the intersections, but signs and signals and well-known landmarks went unnoticed. Instead, her heart beat with the anxiety of a highly charged court case while her mind tore back through the argument, de-emotionalizing it, scrutinizing it, sorting and categorizing each point by its validity.

As in every argument, truth and validity were on both sides, along with enough distortion and exaggeration to push the emotional buttons of hurt and anger. And the chance to answer the whys was overlooked—why they couldn't, or wouldn't, accept each other as they were, embracing differences as well as likeness; why they couldn't put the same effort toward understanding faults as they did toward enjoying attributes; why they should or shouldn't be together.

Isn't answering the whys and turning them into hows what keeps marriages together? Precisely what has kept Anna and Robert Bradley together for thirty-five years? How else could a mixed marriage survive the sixties and nine children and still speak the words I love you without a miss every day of their marriage?

Not until she was past her teens did she begin to realize what a remarkable achievement her parents' marriage was. Now she realized what a monumental achievement such a relationship would be in the gay community. More than once, the possibility had crossed her mind, having a loving, enduring, monogamous relationship with a woman. She examined the possibility, studied what it would take, and just as many times she had dismissed it. For one reason or another, it didn't seem feasible. This time, with Serena, was probably the last time she would even contemplate the idea.

So now what? Shayna watched from her parking space as the young couple from the condo next door unloaded items from their car and teased playfully. Signs of an affectionate making up after last night's differing of opinion that had no doubt been heard by most of Ambrosia Drive's residents. Was it a mutual compromise? Shayna mused. Or did someone give in? They seemed none-the-worse after unloading such anger on each other. Maybe anger had butted against anger in midair and negated its power. No direct hit, no damage?

How would one assess that kind of damage anyway? In the

same way one waits for a judgment in a custody case? Waiting to see if carefully chosen words and relentlessly argued points had struck the heart of the court? Unable to see the effects, unsure of the consequences, waiting hours and sometimes days for what could affect a lifetime.

Well, she wasn't going to wait days, not when she didn't have to. Hours, maybe, long enough for the coals of anger to have cooled, then she'd make amends with Serena and get on with things as usual. Love affairs. Shayna shook her head as she emerged from the car. So unnecessarily complicated.

Seven

"Any challengers today?" Jean asked while the class followed her in the last of their warm-up stretches.

"Yeah." The voice came from the first row of bleachers reserved for those students who were not participating for one reason or another. "If I beat you today, then I'm not going to have to hang around here for the rest of the semester."

Jean held up three fingers to send the class into their warm-up laps, then turned to face Jay Markus's smug smile. "Ah, Mr. Badminton," she declared. "I'm honored. This must mean you're planning on hustling your butt into the locker room and getting dressed for the first time this year."

"Who's gonna break a sweat?"

Her eyes remained on his for a second, maybe two, but it was long enough. He slapped the chest of the boy lounging next to him. "Get me your sweats," he said.

Jean knew before they began how humiliating it would be for him, but she had to let him try. Except for one day when he and a friend had distracted the class by whiffing at the air more than volleying, Jay had virtually no experience with a badminton racket.

After numerous unsuccessful attempts to make contact for a

legal underhand serve, Jay tossed the shuttlecock up and hit it overhand. For the sake of continuance, Jean returned it to his backcourt before he could get his racket up. It was his only chance to serve.

Jean hit two long serves to the back right and left of his service court, then short to the center corner, all untouched. The fourth, a long serve to his forehand side, he hit feebly with the frame of his racket and it fell short of the net. It would be three more serves before he made racket contact again, this time to send the bird limply out of bounds.

His arrogance had spoken over reason and he was making a fool of himself before his classmates, Jean thought. But, to his credit, he did not walk away. He didn't even try to save face with his usual clowning. His smile was gone, his eyes set determinedly. Something had touched a competitive nerve—possibly that Jean had snapped shot after shot exactly where she wanted it. Whatever it was, while some of his classmates cheered and others jeered, Jay stayed his ground. Right up until he finally connected with the middle of his racket and set Jean up with a shot she could not resist. The bird was just high enough and dropping so weakly that without a thought Jean unleashed a full-power smash that unfortunately bulleted the tip of the bird to the crotch of Jay's sweats. He doubled and fell to his knees.

The class exploded in laughter as Jean ducked under the net to apologize. "I'm sorry, Jay. I wasn't trying to hit you."

He rubbed himself as discreetly as possible, then picked up the unexpected source of his pain from in front of him. His quizzical look turned to a smile as he shook his head and stood. "Never thought I'd need a cup for badminton."

"A little practice wouldn't hurt either," Jean returned with a smile.

The challenge was over. The empty court filled quickly with students. Jay picked up the racket, thrust it at his best friend, and turned toward an adjacent court. He shouted so that the little girl on the far side could hear him clearly. "Lezzie Lin, this game almost over?"

Lindy Dae, serious blue eyes peering from between fine strands of honey-brown hair, stopped short of her serve. But before she could respond, Jean's voice rang out from beside the bleachers.

"Jay, I need to talk with you. Over here, please." She waited until they were far enough away from the others before she began. "You know I won't tolerate that in here. Why do you do it?"

"It slipped. It's just a stupid nickname, like Fat Man over there."

He indicated Dan Smythe, who had miraculously embraced the nickname and somehow fashioned acceptance out of embarrassment and discomfort—a mystery Jean had yet to understand. How can some overcome and others not?

"Whether they let on or not, Jay, the names are hurtful to them. Sometimes you can see the pain, sometimes you can't. Those kinds of names are unacceptable, just like some jokes are unacceptable—race jokes, sexist jokes." She hoped the look in her eyes and the tone in her voice had made her point. She lightened her tone. "And blond jokes."

His eyes shifted from watching the students file toward the locker room to resting again on Jean's. "Aw, come on," he said, a smile crinkling around his eyes. "You're a real bore, Mrs. Kesh."

"I've been told that before," she replied. But in so many more words. "Go get dressed."

As soon as she entered the locker room, Jean could see the familiar top of Lindy Dae's head through the large window of her office. She was sitting in the chair opposite the desk with a pencil in one hand and a sandwich in the other, as she did at least three times a week.

Jean sighed and resigned herself to sharing her office and the precious time she had hoped to spend on the phone. Talking to Ken during lunch gave her the perfect excuse for a short conversation. Discussing how to deal with their shared investments tonight could easily turn into a much longer conversation.

Normally she didn't begrudge the time, especially for Lindy, but today she wasn't sure she had the patience. She was making a conscious effort to not give in to the stresses—Ken's repeated requests to work it out, her mother's insistence that she was making a huge mistake, and the school-board's decision to table its judgment indefinitely. Many things unresolved—and possibly irresolvable—and too many days in a row without the reassurance of Shayna's voice. A phone conversation a day with her was becoming a necessity.

"Lindy," Jean began, "is Jay part of the group that's been bothering you?"

It had taken weeks of tactful prodding to uncover why this little apple-pie girl felt the need to hide away in a teacher's office during her lunch period, but the answers came more easily now.

Lindy swallowed her bite of sandwich and nodded.

"Does he say things like that on a regular basis?" She watched Lindy nod again, and refocus on her calculus homework. "Is that why you've been skipping biology class?" Another nod. Jean made a conscious decision to avoid details and moved on. "Why did you skip your appointment with your counselor?" Eye contact again, and mild surprise from Lindy that Jean knew about it. "I spoke with Mrs. Jameson. I think you should give her another chance and go talk with her. Maybe she can switch your classes."

Lindy shook her head. "It'll make things worse, like last time. She pulled some of them out of class and talked to them, and it made it worse."

"Sometimes things have to get worse before they get better. How is she going to effect some change in the situation if she doesn't talk to them?"

"They only laugh at her."

"Then what do you think will help, Lindy? It's all right that you come in here during lunch, but you can't keep skipping classes."

Lindy idly pulled pieces of crust off the remainder of her sandwich and placed them in her lunch sack. Jean waited. She hated watching, day by day, as confusion and fear clouded the bright innocence that once shone from Lindy's eyes. How does one help someone replace lost confidence? Was it possible to encourage someone else to ignore peer pressure and look within for validity when Jean wasn't able to do it for herself?

Lindy spoke quietly. "Mrs. Jameson thinks that I should wear more feminine clothes and—" she spread her fingers through her short hair "—let my hair grow."

The space between Jean's brows knitted into an immediate frown. A Band-Aid for a gaping wound, and it's not even her wound. Not good advice. Despite that first impulse, she glanced at Lindy's jeans and sweatshirt, and chose her words carefully. "That's pretty common attire, though, isn't it?"

Lindy shrugged and refocused on shoving the remainder of her sandwich into her sack. "Do you think I look boyish?"

Thirteen years of teaching made expressionless and tactful responses practically automatic, but being put on the spot was no less uncomfortable. What makes boyish too boyish? And whose judgment should matter? She looked into Lindy's waiting eyes.

"I don't, no. But Mrs. Jameson is trying to find solutions through those kids' eyes." And it's not my place to differ with her. All the classes, all the training for a master's in counseling, and it isn't my place.

"What do you think I should do?" Lindy asked.

Jean leaned forward on folded arms and tilted her head to look directly into Lindy's eyes. "Whenever someone says something cruel, try to keep in mind that everyone has a uniqueness that makes them unlike anyone else. You have thoughts and mannerisms and expressions that make you special, that make you you. And the people that count in your life are those who appreciate that."

"I don't want to be special," she said, staring out into the empty locker room. "I want to be locker eight-two-three-five in a row of empty gray lockers."

Eight

There was no familiar lightness to Serena's voice. It was tight; the ends of her words clipped short. "You gonna be home for the next hour?" There was no indication that Serena's attitude had changed.

Shayna spoke into the phone while retrieving the Jackson case file from her briefcase and dropping it on the coffee table. "Sure. You coming over? I thought you weren't talking to me?"

"I'm just gonna pick up my things."

"Maybe you'll feel more like talking once you get here."

The only response was a dial tone. Shayna frowned and tossed the phone to the end of the couch.

Ten minutes later, Serena was bustling past her and gathering a jacket from the front closet, miscellaneous apparel from the bedroom, and toiletries from the bathroom.

Shayna waited on the couch until the blue nylon bag was filled and dropped at the door and Serena was making a final sweep of the rooms. Shayna had misjudged the situation—something she strove diligently not to do in her professional life. A week, she figured, would have been enough for reconciliation, it should have been. But over two weeks had passed and Serena still buzzed like an angered hornet.

"I am sorry, Serena. Can't we work this out?"

Serena hovered between the coffee table and the entrance hall. "Sorry doesn't change things. I'm sorry it took me this long to figure it out."

"Figure what out?"

"So smart. So damn smart." Serena hung her head and expelled a loud breath. "Big attorney. Figuring out everyone's life except her own."

"I don't un—"

"Proof, right there." Her head snapped up. "I don't understand what you're talkin' about," she mocked.

"Please don't resort to that." Shayna stood and stepped around the table. "Doesn't the past year warrant at least a civil discussion?" She tried unsuccessfully to take Serena's hand.

Tears glazed Serena's eyes and spilled down her cheeks as she spoke. "You're all taken up, baby. Don't you see that? There's no room for me. You go lookin' for custody cases like there's forty hours in a day, like you're gonna save every mother's babies for her. You're hangin' on to me because you hate losin'."

Shayna closed the distance between them and gently grasped the narrow waist. Long hands with their appliqué nails braced themselves against her chest, preventing an embrace.

"What's there left for me? After family—every holiday, every birthday." She pushed against Shayna's chest. "After Jean." The mask of anger that covered what had been too painful for Serena to express began to fall away.

"What do you want me to do, Serena? You don't like my friends, you're uncomfortable around my family."

"What do I have in common with them—a master's degree? Ph.D.? Skin color? What are we gonna talk about? How far we've come from the slave ships?"

"Me, Serena, you have me in common. And a lot of other things if you'd stop being angry long enough to look."

Serena pushed herself clear. "That's what you think? I'm angry?" She shook her head. "No, you don't come from the same place I do, or you'd understand. I've got to worry about grandmas and aunts and cousins and everyone who knows my family. I've got the responsibility of them on me. You don't know what it takes for me to be with you."

"You're letting them live your life for you. They've got chains on you. How can you let your own people do that?"

"My own people—that's what you don't understand. You'll never understand," she shouted, grabbing her bag and whirling toward the door.

"I've tried, Serena," she said as the door bounced back against the stop. "I've tried."

Nine

The large scoreboard high on the north wall of the gym blinked down the seconds to the accompaniment of basketballs pounding a fast path to the basket at either end of the court. Fourteen varsity girls pushed practice-weary legs from one end line to the other in a desperate attempt to score one more fast-break basket than they had the day before. This was their fifth attempt today and unless they scored five more baskets in the next ten seconds, it would not be their last.

Lindy Dae sat at the scorer's table, eyes darting from basket to basket, fingers anxiously clicking the counter button on the scoreboard control. Number fifty-six dropped through the north basket while two in a row missed at the south end.

"Fifty-seven," Lindy counted loudly. "Fifty-eight. Come on, Breeze, Janelle. Fifty-nine. Yes! Two to go. You can do it!"

Coach Porter shouted, "Three seconds."

"Sixty," shouted Lindy. And as sixty-one beat the buzzer at the south end basket, Lindy jumped from her station and rushed onto the court. "Yeah! I knew you could do it," she exclaimed excitedly. She made it a point to high-five each exhausted player and hand her a towel before she collapsed onto the bench.

Lindy could see in their faces that the increasing difficulty of each practice was exactly what Coach Porter intended; it was mimicking the do-or-die level of stress that a winning team must conquer. Nothing must be taken for granted, nothing was a given, not even an uncontested fast-break lay-up.

The players were beginning to understand that. They were going to take the league this year, Lindy was sure of it, and maybe go all the way to the state championship. Besides, they had Janelle Mills, the league's five-foot-nine leading scorer and the most incredible player Lindy had ever seen. It was an honor to be this close, to help the team, to help Janelle any way that she could.

"Janelle, where are you going?" Coach Porter looked up from her free-throw charts as Janelle started for the south gym doors.

Janelle held up a nearly empty water bottle. "I need cold water."

Coach Porter looked toward the corner of the gym entrance where the drinking fountain was and found precisely what she expected, three grinning male faces peering through the narrow windows in the doors. "That's why we have a manager," she replied. And also why she held strictly to her rule of closed practices. High-school girls, she believed, had a hard enough time staying focused.

Lindy grabbed the carriers, and the players dutifully placed their water bottles in them. "I'll hurry," she said, as Janelle reluctantly dropped her bottle in the last empty spot. "Cold water, two minutes."

"Yeah, thanks," Janelle said with a wistful look toward the door. She rolled her eyes at the sound of the coach's voice.

"Free throws," she called. "And they call them that for a reason."

Lindy felt sick to her stomach, she could feel the pulse pounding in her ears as she neared the doors. Her eyes followed the black line outlining the court until it met itself in the corner. She passed the regular drinking fountain with its room temperature water, and continued toward the hall and the refrigerated fountain. It was cold water they deserved and cold they'd get.

She refused to look up even as she pushed her hip against the long handle on the door. As hard as she tried she couldn't take a deep breath, and no matter what she did she wouldn't be able to shut out what she was about to hear.

The door penetrated the group of boys still hovering at the entrance. Lindy squeezed through without making eye contact. She knew their voices by heart now.

Danny Boone. "Hey, Lezzie Lin. I see you're practicin' hard in there with the girls."

Jay Markus. "Yeah, practicin' gettin' close to the girls."

Jason Weeks. "I hear you've been lookin' at my girl in the shower room."

They followed Lindy to the drinking fountain, and Jason continued. "You been lookin' at my girl's tits?"

Lindy swallowed hard and began to fill the water bottles. Perspiration was trickling down her sides. She wanted to run somewhere where she'd never have to see them again. The hand holding the water bottle began to shake.

Jason's voice again. "Answer me, you little pervert." He pushed up against her back and made her drop the bottle. Her forehead banged painfully into the top edge of the stainless-steel fountain, and her eyes filled with tears.

Danny Boone. "Hey, maybe she works up a real sweat so that she can get in there and rub up against 'em."

Jason. "That right? You rubbin' the girls in there?"

The semicircle of boys closed tightly. Lindy could not bend to pick up another bottle without bumping the forest of surrounding legs. She wiped the tears from her eyes and fumbled with the next bottle.

In her head, words shouted to be released. Why are you doing this to me? I've done nothing … I've done nothing. But they stayed locked in her head because once spoken, Lindy knew, they would become sparks on tinder. The only control she had was in not making the situation worse. She thought about the side door exit only a few yards away, of pushing through the boys and making her escape. She could run to her car and race home to the safety of her room. She could close her door and close her mind, and play her music until the tears stopped and she fell asleep.

But she had promised the team, and she was already taking too long. She ignored the questions the best she could.

"What else you wanna do to them?"

"You don't get off just watchin', do ya?"

Lindy struggled to fight her own fears.

"She wants to lick 'em where we stick 'em." The words echoed, in the hall, in her mind. She pushed through the laughing boys and their groping hands and scrambled toward the gym as quickly as her burden would allow. Once inside, she wiped her eyes once more, then hurried toward the bleachers.

Marlene Dae spoke through her daughter's closed bedroom door. "Honey, I warmed up some stroganoff and homemade bread. You really should try to eat. Please, honey, it'll make you feel better."

Nothing would really make her feel better. Her favorite food, her favorite music, even her sweet Greta cuddling and purring against the back of her neck couldn't heal the pain in her heart. Lindy wiped her face on her pillow and answered her mother.

"I'm not hungry. Let me be, Mom. I've got a lot of home-work to do." She rolled onto her back, gently forcing Greta to reposition herself on the pillow.

Marlene lowered her eyes and retreated slowly down the old spiral-rail stairway. She seemed oblivious to its familiar creaks and groans.

John Dae looked up from the sports page in time to recognize the look on his wife's face as she passed toward the kitchen. The dinner tray she carried was untouched. He sighed and dropped the paper next to the chair.

"It's those kids again, isn't it?" he asked.

The concern was evident in her eyes. "She won't tell me anymore. I think she's afraid I'll go to the school again."

John rose and started toward the stairs. "It wouldn't do any good. They think you're a fanatic, an overprotective parent."

"This isn't right, John. She should be staying out too late with friends and getting grounded and making us wish she had her own phone." She looked back up the stairs. "This isn't right."

John patted his wife's shoulder. "I'll go talk to her."

He sat on the edge of the bed, his arm around his daughter, large thick fingers gently smoothing her hair. He had helped to raise three other children, two now married with their own children, and another about to graduate from college. But nothing in raising them had prepared him for this. He and Marlene had dealt with speeding tickets and teen-aged drinking, petty theft, and the fear of unwanted pregnancy. Yet in every case, he'd had the sense that they could round the corner even if it was on two wheels.

But Lindy had been different right from the beginning.

She was their change-of-life baby, their unexpected blessing. They were nearly as unprepared for her birth as he was at this moment. He would give almost anything to be able to take away her pain. If only he knew how.

"You can't let them get you down like this, angel," he said with a kiss to her head. "They keep it up when they know they're getting to you."

"I try," she said, sitting up out of his embrace. "Every day I try."

"There was this kid when I was in high school—" he chuckled "—Donny Belzar." It was all that came to mind. "We sure gave ol' Donny a tough way to go. Me and Grayson and Big John. We chased him home every day, tripped him, threw rocks at his legs. He sure didn't like us much."

Even with all the stories of childhood mischief he had shared with her, this one surprised Lindy. As big and gruff as he looked, he was a man who couldn't even hunt a rabbit, a man who had taught her to carve delicate sculptures out of Ivory soap. How could this man have been a bully? "Why did you hate him, Dad?"

"That's just it—we didn't hate Donny, we kinda felt sorry for him." Another chuckle. "Until our senior year, anyway."

"What happened?"

"He gave us religion. During the summer between his junior and senior years he worked on his uncle's farm. The first day of school, we couldn't believe it was the same kid. He was all muscled out on his chest and back, and his deltoids looked like quarterback pads." He smiled and shook his head. "We were still cocky, though, and stupid. Grayson opened his big mouth in the locker room and said something—I don't remember what it was, but it was something that we usually got away with—and that really ticked ol' Donny off. Before I could even blink, Donny's fist had flown past my face. It grazed right here—" he brushed his fingers over the top of his ear "—then slammed into the door of the locker and caved it in like it was made out of cardboard." He blew a soft whistle. "Damn, that boy would've killed me if he'd hit me."

Lindy smiled. "How's that supposed to help me, Dad?"

"Well—" he was sure it had been obvious "—things change. They won't treat you like that forever."

"But what if they don't change, and I don't either? What if they're right?"

He had come to the end of his own confidence. No specifics came to mind. He was left with what his own father had said to him on more than one occasion. "Everything will be all right, you'll see. Things have a way of working themselves out. You'll just have to give it time." Pitifully lame and wholly inadequate, he had to admit, but it was the best he could do.

The pictures covered the wall above her bed—Breeze, dribbling a ball with each hand, Janelle wearing her favorite baseball cap, Sky shooting free throws at an early morning two-a-day practice still dressed in her nightgown and slippers. The sight made her laugh despite how miserable she felt. In the middle of the dozen-plus candids was the official team photo—her team. Looking at it filled her with pride. It was okay that she wasn't tall enough or fast enough to play with them; they were still her team. They needed her, and she took very good care of them.

She studied the picture more thoroughly than usual, past the laughter and the obvious, into their eyes and wondered if the memories were all hers. If she were gone, would they miss her as much as she would miss them?

Ten

The café had an air of bohemian artiness. Intimate round tables crowded the large front window, while a local group played a strange mix of jazz and rhythm-and-blues from a room deep in its interior. A semi-secluded niche in the middle of the café offering mix-and-matched overstuffed chairs, warm and glowing golden from the heat of a gas-log fireplace, had become their favorite meeting place every Wednesday and Friday.

Already settled with a cup of her favorite coffee, Jean watched the ever-interesting clientele and waited for Shayna. Small groups of university students followed the music toward the back and disappeared. The gay men's chorus, chatty and exuberant from rehearsal, began lining up at the front counter to place their orders from the vegetarian menu on the wall. The little tables near the window filled quickly.

Jean liked it here. It was a slip of space she could share with Shayna, a coveted slice of time they could devote to the needs of the moment. Nothing was ever too trivial to talk about or too complex to tackle. They bounced theories and ideas off each other without reservation. They shared thoughts with no fear of rejection and teased each other without fear of insult.

Their friendship, having evolved from a favor for a friend, had exceeded all Jean's expectations. Shayna had devoted time to advising Katherine on her university problems, and that time, when no longer needed by Katherine, had become time for advice for one of Jean's students. And when the time was no longer needed by the student, it became personal time for the two of them. They shopped and went to movies and tried out new weekend lunch spots.

Now, the friendship that had garnished the edges of her marriage had put down roots in the cavities of her separation and blossomed on its own. Its day-by-day growth, like the unfolding of a flower, had occurred practically unnoticed until suddenly it was unavoidably bright and beautiful and an important part of each day.

Jean turned off her cell phone and tucked it neatly into the pocket of her bag. The only rule for their evenings was no phone calls.

"How many people did you have to kick out of my chair?" Shayna asked as she passed behind Jean.

Jean breathed in the familiar scent that lately sent little electrical charges jumping every synapse in her system. She took another quick breath while the scent lingered. "There was only that frail old homeless man who looked about frozen … oh, and the old lady looking for a cushy seat because of her hip replacement. I let them know that this seat was reserved."

Shayna smiled. "I'm sorry I'm late. I had to wait for a call from the psychologist." She handed Jean a fresh cup of cafe latté and her favorite raspberry torte. "You won't hear me admit this often, but this case has me worried."

"The lesbian mother?"

Shayna answered with a nod and a sigh of exasperation. She rested her head on the back of the chair and closed her eyes.

"You look tired."

"You know how it used to feel when you'd have a big pimple starting under the surface and your skin hurt all around the area, but you couldn't pinpoint where it would erupt?"

Jean smiled. "Imbued in my mind forever."

"That's how this case feels. There's something ugly under the surface and I can't find it and I'm running out of time."

"When's the hearing?"

"Next Wednesday, and we drew Judge Hobarth." She shook her head slowly. "A son of a bitch who hides his prejudices behind a black robe instead of a white one. I have to find something wrong with those kids living with their father, and it has to be so blatant that even Hobarth can't give him custody."

"You must have some suspicion. What do you think the situation is?"

"Not only is Justice supposed to be blindfolded, but she also has selective hearing. She doesn't hear thoughts or suspicions, she hears only facts. The best I can do is make what meager facts I have as sympathetic to the court as possible."

"Then what do you know?"

Shayna puffed her cheeks and blew the air out slowly. "I know I have a young mother struggling at minimum wage to take care of two kids. I have a well-behaved, amazingly well-adjusted seven-year-old boy who seems to be equally comfortable with both his mother and his father. I have an angry, sometimes violent five-year-old girl who hates going to her father's but sometimes makes her mother's life miserable. And I have a father who looks squeaky clean—good job, new wife, nice house, and some mysterious way of controlling the five-year-old."

"Let me guess," Jean interjected. "He's using the little girl's behavior as proof that living with a lesbian mother is screwing her up."

"Among other things." Shayna leaned forward, embracing her cappuccino with both hands. "In the year and a half that they've been divorced, he's threatened to haul her into court for not providing receipts for everything his monthly pittance was spent on, insinuating that it wasn't spent on the kids, and for having women stay at the house. He pumps the kids for information every time he gets them, then makes accusations about showing affection in front of them or saying something inappropriate. The kids are starting to clam up around everyone; they don't know what to say. The poor mother has no kind of a life left. She won't even leave the kids with a baby-sitter for fear of false accusations, and she can't leave them with her own family because they support him."

"But she has the best custody attorney in the state fighting for her." Jean tried to sound reassuring despite what seemed an insurmountable task. "You told me once that dead ends are just places to trap someone. So which dead end looks most promising?"

"The kids, particularly the boy."

"Why?"

"The little girl has completely shut down. She tells everyone, 'I don't want to talk to you.' Plus, there are too many variables that could be causing her to act out."

"Her age, her parents constantly arguing, insecurity," Jean concluded.

"Maybe if I can figure out why the boy is so much better behaved, why he has no problem going to Dad's."

Without hesitation, Jean replied, "Maybe they're treated differently—different rules, different expectations. Kids feel the unfairness and eventually there is rebellion of some sort. We spent a lot of time on this in one of my grad classes. I paid close attention because I'd seen the impact that differential treatment had in education."

Shayna made a quick mental search of the psychologist's report she'd reread just a couple of hours earlier. In all the observations and jargon, there hadn't been one possibility that suggested what Jean so easily surmised. A smile eased across Shayna's face. "Now I suppose you're going to want a raise, and since an assistant of your caliber is hard to come by, I'll have to give it to you."

Jean felt her face flush. "Did that help?"

"It has me taking a fresh look at that cul-de-sac through someone else's eyes, those of a little boy who the psychologist says has a strong need to please. As soon as I get home, I'll read the reports again."

"The psychologist didn't suggest that that was a possibility?"

"The father has refused to come to the counseling sessions. The mother treats them equally, and the kids aren't talking, so the psychologist has nothing to base that assumption on. She can't report what she doesn't know. You and I, though, can assume anything we want if it helps us get at the truth."

"Kids actually speak quite clearly; we simply have to learn how to hear what they're saying. They're creative—we lose much of that creativity by the time we reach adulthood. Lindy Dae, the student I told you about?"

Shayna nodded.

"She's a perfect example. She won't talk with the counselor any more, so I took a look through her file. There was an exercise in there from her third-grade teacher. It was a series of drawings Lindy made of a child doing various things like riding a bike, playing ball, throwing a stick for a dog, mostly by herself. The other people in the pictures seemed to be unconnected, not interacting with the child—except for one picture where the child is holding hands with what I assume are parents. But what is most strange about the pictures is that there is all this detail, buttons on clothing, a watch on the father, a collar on the dog, yet the child has no face. In all of the pictures—just a blank face—no eyes, no nose, no mouth."

The space between Shayna's brows pushed into a dark line. "Third grade? How did school personnel interpret that?"

"Self-esteem problems. Teachers were encouraged to give her additional responsibilities and to praise her accomplishments more consistently. Oftentimes kids like her blend into the woodwork. The exceptionally outgoing and the problematic kids get all the attention."

"But you think it was deeper than that?"

Jean nodded. "Yes, I do. Those pictures Lindy drew say even more about her now as a teenager. She's confused about her identity, and she's been telling people about it for a long time. But when adults stopped listening, Lindy stopped talking."

"Until now, until you."

Jean tilted her head. "I'm doing my best."

"So am I, but sometimes it takes more than trying. Losing this case is not an option. I've got to talk to the little boy again." Shayna leaned forward into a longer-than-usual gulp of coffee, indicating that the anxiety she felt was about to make this a short evening.

Before Shayna could reach for her briefcase, though, Jean quickly changed the subject. "I hate to ask this because I know this is a tough week for you." She watched Shayna take another deep gulp and place the cup on the table with a final clink. "Could you maybe spare an hour or two to help me move some furniture? An upstairs apartment is available, and I'm going to grab it. I can't take that guy stomping around up there and the bed frame bouncing all night. I'd ask Ken, but things have been rather touchy lately."

"He hasn't had enough time to adjust, has he?"

"No, and I finally said the word that had to be said."

"The D word."

Jean nodded. "I can hardly ask him to help me make this more permanent."

"Like making a kid go fetch the belt that's going to put welts on his hind end."

"My parents used to say, 'You don't understand it now, but this is really for your own good. Someday you'll see that.'"

"Were they right?"

Jean smiled slightly and shook her head. "Not in every case. This, though, I know is best for him."

"I hope so," Shayna replied. "If you can wait until after the hearing, I'll give you all the hours you need."

Eleven

The room was still, cavern-like, completely dark and isolated. Nothing beyond the walls, nothing beyond the darkness. Shayna's thoughts echoed in the stillness, competing with the sound of her own heartbeat.

He has just been there, only a moment ago, jumping on the sofa, laughing, and racing just out of her reach. This was the time that she could see him and hear him, alone in the middle of the night. She could feel the pangs of panic all over again, as if for the first time. Her heart raced. Her eyes, wide and unblinking, stared into the darkness and saw only her own fear, fear so debilitating that it eliminated all reasoning. She did not remember that there was nothing more to do, nothing more to fear. He was there and small, and so was she.

But in the next moment she knew Benny was gone—little boy, little brother—forever. He would never again frustrate her or bother her or make her laugh. Shayna sat up abruptly. "He's gone," she whispered into the darkness. She threw the covers to the other side of the bed. There's nothing I can do now.

The only way she knew to fight the panic was to get up. Be in the light; be busy. It was her adult substitution for the sounds of a large family that had always comforted her as a child. Even late at night she had known she wasn't alone. There were muffled footsteps and muted voices, music and laughter, and the deep breathing of a sleeping sibling. Always the sense of someone near to buffer the painful thoughts and chase the monsters from under the bed so that she could sleep.

Now the monsters were her responsibility. She grabbed a pair of sweats from the end of the bed, left the monsters in the dark, and started for the kitchen. She warmed a cup of leftover coffee in the microwave oven, then settled on the couch to lose herself in the pages of the Jackson case.

The night brought on doubt. She questioned everything, from her own analysis of the case and her ability to argue it, to the accuracy of the facts and their effect on the court. Nothing was left to chance. Her thumbprint would be on every page, every word, every thought involved with the case. Dana Jackson and her children would get her very best, because what Shayna Bradley feared most was failing another child.

Twelve

Dana Jackson sighed as she stooped to retrieve the plastic horses her daughter had just thrown across the room.

The little voice screamed at the top of its range, "I don't have to do what you tell me."

Dana closed her eyes and took a deep breath. Then she stood and tossed the toys back on the floor. "No, you don't. You don't have to pick up your things or brush your teeth or do anything. You can go to bed in your dirty clothes right now."

"No!" she screamed back.

Dana took another deep breath to bolster her patience before replying, "I'm going to have your brother pick out a book for us to read before bed. I hope you'll be able to join us because it won't be special without you. But unless you pick up your things and—"

"Nooo." The loud protest was followed by the little body streaking across the room, slamming into Dana's legs, and knocking her to the floor.

"Stop it!" Dana demanded, trying to catch hold of the tiny fists swinging at her face. "Stop it right now!" She finally captured both arms, forced them to her daughter's sides, and pulled her under one arm. She stood and carried her daughter to the bedroom, despite frantic kicks to her leg. She shut the door and returned to the living room.

Dana collapsed on the couch and covered her face with her hands. She tried to fight back the tears, tried not to cry in front of her son. But it was no use.

He placed the book on her lap and snuggled up beside her.

"Don't cry, Mom. Please, don't cry." The cries from the other room could be heard over the kicking and pounding on the bedroom door. Tears worked their way down his mother's cheeks.

"I'll tell you a secret," he said, scrambling to his knees so that he could whisper in her ear. "Tell her you'll take her to Uncle Aaron's."

Dana wiped the tears from her face, and slicked the hair from her son's forehead with a wet palm. "I'm okay, sweetie," she said, hugging him tightly to her. "See? I stopped crying."

He seemed pleased that what he said had worked so well.

But Dana didn't really understand. "Why should I tell her that?"

"Because she'll stop acting up." He put his finger to his lips and hushed his tone. "If she doesn't stop, Dad takes her there and leaves her overnight."

Dana sat straight up and looked seriously into his eyes. "Is that the secret? Did someone tell you that it's a secret?"

He nodded, his eyes wide.

"Who, sweetie? Who told you to keep it a secret?"

He cupped his hand around her ear and leaned in to whisper, "Grandpa Jackson."

Her own voice was just above a whisper. "Is Grandpa Jackson staying at Uncle Aaron's?"

He nodded. Dana bolted from the couch, grabbed the phone, and rushed to her bedroom. Her hand was shaking. She had to dial the number twice. Please pick up, please. "Shayna, this is Dana. I'm very confused and worried right now, and we need to talk."

Thirteen

The old two-story colonial on Third Street had seen its share of changes over the years. The wood-framed screens had been replaced with modern storms, and white vinyl siding now saved Robert Bradley and his boys from uncounted hours of scraping and painting. The biggest changes, however, had taken place in the lives of the family that had grown within its walls.

Cars lined both sides of the narrow neighborhood street. The entire family had gathered as expected. Shayna's two older brothers would by now be thoroughly engrossed in a heated debate with the twins over John Rocker's value to baseball. Her baby sister would be throwing a barrage of questions about campus life at her two college sisters. Their patience, Shayna suspected, would be waning about now.

Shayna knew her family well; she'd paid close attention after Bennie died. More closely than most eight-year-olds usually found need to pay, and probably too close at times. But she had made a promise, a little girl's promise to her mother and to God, and she had done everything that she could to fulfill it. She would be the best little girl she could be so that nothing bad would ever happen to her family again. She took on the responsibilities of a teenager, helping to cook and clean and watch after her siblings. To this day, it has been the most important promise she has ever made. Even now, it was rare that she didn't know where each of her seven brothers and sisters was and what they were doing. Miraculously, none of them seemed to have retained any long-term disdain for their sister as parent.

The immediate Bradley family was large by most standards, but added to it were three wives, two boyfriends, six grandchildren, and three dogs, and the house and backyard were overflowing in a fitting tribute to Anna and Robert's thirty-fifth wedding anniversary.

Shayna made her way through the throng, loud with laughter and debate, hugging and greeting, and skirting racing children and dogs until she spotted her mother coming out of the kitchen. Shayna took the platter of appetizers from her mother's hands and handed it to a passing sister-in-law. "This is exactly why we had this shindig catered," Shayna said with a smile. She kissed her mother's forehead, wrapped her arms around her, and squeezed the tiny frame gently.

As a teenager, she had worried how a woman so slight could make love with such a large man and not be crushed beneath him, and wondered how it was possible for her to have safely birthed so many big babies. Now she understood not only her mother's strength but also appreciated her father's gentleness. "Happy anniversary, Mom. Where can I find the big guy responsible for this zoo?"

Anna's face burst into a smile surrounded by a series of crescent-shaped creases, the result of too many hours in the sun early in her marriage. Years in Shayna's childhood when she could remember her mother being as dark-skinned as her father. At the time she didn't understand why. "Careful now," Anna returned. "That's my best beau you're talking about."

"After all of this?" A rambunctious six-year-old squealed and squeezed between Shayna's legs in an effort to avoid his pursuer. "And he's still your best beau? Well, Mother Teresa had nothing on you."

Anna slapped her playfully on the arm. "He's out back, trying to round everyone up to eat." Not a surprise. They could never eat soon enough for Robert Bradley.

Shanya found him shooing a large Australian shepherd, intent on digging up Anna's cherished bulbs, from the garden. "Get your hiney outta there, or we'll both pay dearly."

"Guaranteeing yourself another anniversary?"

"Aha," he laughed, straightening and grabbing Shayna in a bear hug. "Here's my girl. Just in time to save me from starvation. Your momma wouldn't let us eat until you got here."

She patted her dad's pronounced middle. "Oh, you had a couple more hours of life left here."

He laughed heartily as Shayna slipped her monthly college-fund check into his hand. Ten percent from each working sibling to guarantee a college education for the next in line—twenty percent from Shayna. "Honey," he said with a shake of his head, "this is the only thing I've ever kept from your momma. You either have to stop doing this or you have to let me tell her."

"Let it be, Dad. Mom doesn't need to know that I'm putting in Bennie's ten percent, it'll just make her think about it all over again every month. It's something I need to do, and I don't want any analysis from the doctor, please. After dinner, though, I could use some advice."

He draped his arm across her shoulders and slipped the check in his pocket.

Despite huge wet snowflakes laying a quickly melting blanket of white over the lawn, the touch football game began with after-dinner enthusiasm. Neither size nor sex made any difference in this game with its ever-changing ground rules. Even the dogs were allowed to run interference. On any other occasion Shayna, too, would be right in the midst of the fun instead of watching from the window of the den. Today, though, whatever insight Robert Bradley might be able to offer far outweighed anything else.

"I am a blessed man," he said, easing into his chair and gazing out the window past Shayna. "A loving woman, lots of beautiful children—good children who make me as proud as any man on earth."

Shayna smiled. He was a huge man with a heart that filled his chest and a hand that guided his babies from the day they could walk. A father who taught his children the meaning of Ralph Waldo Emerson's words: "What lies behind us and what lies before us are tiny matters compared to what lies within us." A social worker with a caseload of kids, some of whom sparked his anger and many who saddened his heart.

Consciously or not, he had created his own little society, one that gave him balance and a sense of normalcy. His children, unlike those he worked with each day, had tested for boundaries and found them, had asked for guidance and received it, had needed love and never had to ask for it. Shayna truly understood his blessing.

"I see kids torn apart by divorce and I realize how blessed my life has been."

He nodded his head in that knowing manner that had always been a comfort to her, especially during the tough time when the fragility of life was a lesson she wasn't ready to learn.

"So what has you so bothered that you can't enjoy a little football?"

"A couple of things, one professional and the other personal." Her trust in him went beyond his experience in social work, beyond the intelligence it took for a doctorate; it went as far back as she could remember. To her father lifting her high to rest against his shoulder, her aching body wrought with fever, his strong arms carrying her, holding her safe until he had to relinquish his hold to the doctor. A trust that had been later tried and proven during the tough time, after Bennie died and her father's grief was nearly as immeasurable as her own. Enduring together a test of love and faith for which she still dared question God's purpose. The problems they would discuss today paled by comparison. Yet, she knew he would advise her as though world peace depended on his answers.

"The Jackson case, the case you wanted Jane Cooley in on?" he asked.

"Yes, and Jane's as good as you said, but it may not be enough for Judge Hobarth. She was able to loosen the little boy up enough for him to say that he is always good at his dad's so that he doesn't have to go to his uncle's like his sister. And get this," she added, "he gets to have his own room when she's at the uncle's, while his sister has to share a room with the grandfather."

The look in his eyes told her what she already knew. "Boy, I don't like that," he stated. "What's the girl saying?"

"Nothing. As good as Jane is, she couldn't get her to open up at all. Just 'I don't want to talk to you' and then she'd hurl the doll across the room. My suspicions are only that, Dad. I can't prove sexual abuse, and that's the only thing that I think would give me a chance with this judge."

"Why is the girl being sent to another relative's house during the father's visitation?"

"According to the little boy, that's his dad's way of dealing with her behavior. And Dana suspects that it's his way of trying to keep peace with his new wife."

"Does she want the kids?"

"She signed the statement with her husband and seems to be supporting him."

"But?"

"But she's made statements to the mother that make me think that she's more concerned about helping him get the kids away from a lesbian mother. Comments like, 'You've disrupted my life enough, the least you could do is get the kids here on time.' Hardly concrete evidence."

"Things are rarely concrete when it comes to divorces and custody and raising kids."

"I need your take on it, Dad."

"You've set up a schedule for the mother and kids to work with Jane on a continuing basis?" He watched his daughter nod, and continued. "The father made any attempt at counseling with his daughter?"

"No, he blames the problems on the mother's lifestyle and lack of parenting skills. He claims things will be different once the daughter's living with normal parents."

"All I can do is affirm what you already know. You have statistics and psychological consensus that support keeping the children with their mother as long as there is no neglect or abuse. The mother has made efforts that put the kids first—counseling, sacrificing her personal life—while the father's putting himself and his marriage first. It comes down to one man's belief as to whether or not a lesbian mother can raise healthy, well-adjusted kids, and whether you can convince him of that."

"Whether a black woman can convince him of that."

"You were raised without excuses, don't look for any now."

"No excuses." He needn't remind her. He had set an example that would never be forgotten. She had watched him for years, assessing situations, analyzing people, figuring out what was required of him. There was no cruising speed, no automatic in his life, only a constant shifting of the gears. He worked longer, tried harder, and learned more, whatever it took to get where he wanted to be. The only time he could stop shifting was when he came home. He had taught her well. "I just want to know what gear I need to be in."

"Stories about Hobarth's personal beliefs abound throughout the county building. From the bench—" he cocked his head and lifted the corner of his mouth with a clicking sound "—he's all over the board. I've been in the courtroom when he's looked into the tearful eyes of a black mother and told her to take her son home and make sure he never ends up in his court again. The boy could've done jail time. I've also seen him award custody of a child to the paternal grandmother because he said the mother chose to take college classes that take time away from her daughter."

"That one hit the media, I remember it. It's on appeal, isn't it?"

"He has an embarrassingly high reversal rate on appeals."

Shayna took a deep breath and released it audibly.

"You've had your share of tough cases, Riki-Tiki. You know what you have to do. Strike the back of the skull and hang on until it's over." He hesitated until her eyes were squarely on his, then patted his hand over his heart. "There's something in here that's got you bothered even more."

"Not more. It's a different kind of unrest. A friend has asked me to handle her divorce."

He pressed the right side of his face forward and waited for the real punch line.

Shayna obliged. "There is a conflict of interest that I don't think she is aware of."

"Did you advise the divorce?"

"No. I've tried not to influence her decision."

"Then you and she both know there is no conflict, and you're not one to worry that others may think so." He looked directly into her eyes. "In all the miles and the places that our emotional roads have taken us, we've never gone here before, have we?"

His wisdom still amazed her. "This place had never been there before."

Robert nodded. "So. You're in love with her," he said, "but you haven't told her."

"This isn't like anything else I've experienced. She's allowed me into the private places of her life, and I can't leave."

"'Are you afraid to let her into yours?"

"Yes, sir, I am. I feel like I would be opening an empty reservoir to a rushing river. I wouldn't be able to stop it."

"The scariest part of life is that which we cannot control. And love, in this man's opinion, is as scary as it gets. You can't control love in your own heart, and you certainly can't control it in someone else's."

"But I can control risking a friendship that's been four years in the making by not saying those three simple words."

He looked closely into his daughter's eyes. It was all there, the same need, the same fear to satisfy it that he had felt all those years ago. "I wonder where I'd be right now had I not risked saying those words. Would I be an unhappy man? An angry man? What would it have taken to numb my heart?"

"How did you know to risk it?"

He lifted his eyes to the ceiling. When they returned to hers, he said, "I don't think I knew, not then. I only knew that a friendship wasn't enough. I wanted to share all my life with her, and I couldn't do that as only a friend. In my youthful naiveté, I think I was looking for permanence. My parents were married all my life, so I saw marriage as the way to keep her in my life."

"And if she had rejected your love, wouldn't you be in the same place had you not told her?"

He shook his head. "Unrequited love asks questions of you that no other situation does. They go to the heart of your soul and question its worth."

"You loved her enough to risk that?"

Robert smiled. "I like to think I knew her heart well enough, but I was really just floating around in a love-tinted bubble, unaware of how easily it could have burst."

Love-tinted bubble or not, Shayna admired what it must have taken for her parents to have even dated in the early sixties, to say nothing of the strength of love it took to make their marriage successful. Nothing, however, in her own life had given her any hope of experiencing the same kind of long-term love. A commitment that shared days and nights with the only person to whom one has devoted love and loyalty—the person in whom one has entrusted every secret, every fear. The kind of love that endures disagreements and hurt only to return each time to warm nights wrapped securely in the other's arms. Such a hope, she feared, may be just too painful. At least work-driven days and lonely nights were manageable.

Shayna offered him a close-lipped smile. "Handle her divorce?"

He replied, "Handle your heart."

Fourteen

Jean finished the hamstring stretches along with the class, then broke into a run to lead the warm-up laps. Jay Markus finished only steps behind her. Before she could catch her breath, he handed her a badminton racket.

The final week of any physical education unit demanded a certain type of energy from the students and the teacher. An acceptable level of performance was expected from each student, and an expected measure of fairness in evaluating her students' progress was expected from the teacher.

Individual effort was clearly a large part of the evaluation, and the amount needed from each student varied from unit to unit. Few units, however, demanded physically what this one did from the teacher. This one, this year, had taxed Jean more than any other ever had.

Most students had made sporadic attempts to beat her over the weeks, but they had soon stopped, preferring to practice or challenge another student instead. Some never challenged her at all. Jay Markus, however, had been relentless in his pursuit of victory. He had dressed for class, led warm-up exercises, and challenged Jean every day that she would allow it.

Despite how miserably he had lost in the beginning, he never gave up. Somewhere during the middle weeks of the unit, his skills began to improve noticeably. His serves became less predictable, his strokes more consistent. His defensive coverage of the court could now bring him back from the brink of defeat. Beating him was no longer a given.

They used a volley for a warm-up, and that had become a game in itself, lasting up to a dozen shots before one of them erred. The beginning of today's game, and Jay's last chance for victory, was no exception. He had kept his shots low and wide, avoiding Jean's deadly smash, and finally won the serve by tapping a hairpin shot barely over the net that Jean refused to dive for.

He took a deep breath and positioned himself in the front inside corner of the service court. "You ready?" he asked. "Because today you lose."

"Serve" was her only reply.

It was a deep serve toward the center of her court. Jean returned it with a roundhouse deep to his left, forcing him to backpedal for a backhand. As anticipated, his return was short and to Jean's right. She reached it in time to send a well-placed drop over the center of the net. Long limbs stretched to their limit but kept Jay on his feet and out of the net. He managed a weak defensive shot that Jean easily tapped out of his reach.

No score—Jean's serve. She kept it short and low, forcing him to lift it to her forehand. She hit a hard shot crosscourt; he snapped a hard return. Stopping short on her follow-through, she sent a soft shot that dropped quickly in front of him. He hit defensively; contact without the impetus to clear it behind her. The shuttlecock hung above her as he braced for the smash he knew was coming. But there was no defense for it. It hit him squarely in the chest before he could get his racket on it. One-love.

A deep serve to his backhand was cleared, a clear to his right returned, a hard drive to his short left court returned to hit the top of the net and topple over. It landed on the boundary line and gave the serve to Jay.

The game continued in the same hard-fought manner, the

serve often changing sides of the court two or three times before a point was scored. When they were scored, the points usually came at the end of long rallies. Weariness was causing some shots to go wide of the boundary, others to be timed poorly and land in the net. Still others came more quickly off indefensible smashes and serves wide and long of the service court.

They battled to a ten-point tie past the end of the class period and were ten minutes into the lunch period. Neither held a lead of more than one point. The crowd of students watching had diminished sharply at the bell with assurances that those remaining would shout loud enough to be heard in the cafeteria should Jay win.

They had seen love-all three times with neither of them able to put together two points in a row for the win. Sweat had soaked a dark triangle from the neck of Jean's T-shirt. Jay's shirt had long since been tossed to the sideline. Off balance shots and net toppers were telltale signs of weariness, but neither student nor teacher was about to give in.

Jean wiped sweat from her face with her sleeve, then wiped the grip of her racket with bottom of her shirt. She looked across the net at the spaces now, not her opponent. She mapped a strategy, leaned forward, and delivered a short serve to the inside corner of Jay's left service court. Jay succeeded in keeping his return low, but not away from Jean's forehand. She powered a long risky drive to the back right corner of Jay's court. Out of reach for tired legs, the bird dropped untouched just inside the boundary. Advantage Jean.

Her next strategy already set in her mind, she took her position and delivered another short serve to the inside corner which caught Jay back on his heels, expecting a long serve. He corrected in time to make enough contact with the tip of his racket to get the bird back over the net, but it was too high. Jean had ample time to direct a perfect cross-court drop. Jay dove to his left, his full five-foot-eleven frame extended parallel to the floor, landing in a bare-chested skid. The head of his racket rested on the floor only inches from the motionless bird.

He dropped his forehead to the floor. The gasps and groans from onlookers couldn't hide his frustration. "Fuck!" He blurted.

"I'm going to ignore that—" Jean chuckled and ducked under the net "—because I'm too tired to do anything about it."

He turned over with a groan and rubbed his chest. "Are you okay?" she asked.

"All that," he grumbled, "for nothing'."

"What do you mean for nothing? Look what you've learned."

"Yeah, that sometimes things just ain't what they look like. But, I still lost," he complained, pulling himself slowly to his feet.

"And you earned yourself an A doing it. Don't you realize what an awesome player you've become?"

"Yeah?" He smiled as he rubbed his chest.

"Yeah. You're awesome. Now go get dressed."

She was gathering the rackets from the floor when, without warning, someone lifted her shirt from behind and placed something ice cold against her lower back. Jean gasped and spun around to face Brian's grin and a Diet Coke.

"I bet this would taste good about now," he said, opening the can and handing it to Jean.

"Inappropriate, Brian." She held the can to her face, then took a long drink. "But thanks."

"Had to come see this for myself. The guys have been waggin' about this for weeks."

"So what do you think?"

"A pair of shorts and a sweaty T-shirt can be sexy."

Jean rolled her eyes. "About Jay."

"Oh, yeah." He grinned. "Pretty amazing, actually. I wouldn't have believed it without seeing it."

"If he'd put that kind of effort toward his other classes, he'd have a four-point."

Brian smirked. "Never gonna happen. You just touched a sensitive nerve in his budding manhood, that's all."

"Don't be so skeptical." She twirled the racket in front of him. "You didn't believe this could happen."

He took the racket from her and waved it back and forth. "How can you hit something so hard with something this light?"

"Hey, what do you know about Jay and the group he hangs with?"

"They're all jocks, even most of the girlfriends. I've got Danny Boone and Jason Weeks in auto shop. Had a couple of the others last year." He picked up the bird and tapped it over the net. "If they had to list their priorities in life, they would be beer, sex, the sport they're in, and how to keep their grades high enough to stay eligible for the sport they're in, in that order."

"I suspected as much."

"Candidates for retroactive birth control as far as I'm concerned."

Jean smiled. "That bad?"

"Their brains have less convulsions than a bowling ball. They're fuck-ups, and someday they're really gonna fuck up."

"They've been picking on Lindy Dae."

"Yesterday it was the fat boy, today it's Lindy, tomorrow it's some other poor schmuck. Anyone unlike themselves was put on this earth for their amusement."

"What do you do to stop it?"

"Me personally? If I hear it, I drag the class into the classroom and give 'em my consideration-of-others lecture. They shut up because they'll do anything to stay out of the classroom. I doubt if it has any long-term effect."

"So much depends on what they go home to. What do you know about their home life?"

"Danny Boone's new this year. I only met his parents once. Average middle class, seem concerned enough about their kids. Jay Markus's mother works at the bowling alley lounge. She kicked her ol' man out last year after she finally caught him with the neighbor's baby-sitter."

"I've had quite a lot of contact with Jay's mother. He schmoozes her like he does everyone else. I think she sees in him the good things she used to see in his father, and she's not ready to lose that too. So she lets him schmooze. How about Jason Weeks? Isn't it his father who always shows up drunk at the games?"

"Yeah, he's real fun to deal with even when he's sober. He's the kind of parent that never shows up for student conferences, but as soon as there is any kind of discipline involving his boys, he's right in your face screamin' about how you have no right to treat his kids that way. Remember the couple that got into a knock-down-drag-out-fight in the parking lot after the homecoming game? Mr. and Mrs. Weeks."

"Speaks volumes."

"Yup," he said, handing her the racket and starting a bow-legged stride toward the door. "Not much we can do about that."

Fifteen

Shayna remained slumped into the large pillows at the end of the couch, where she'd been for over an hour. Closing her eyes and burying her face didn't stop the words from reverberating in her head. Custody is hereby remanded to William Jackson … William Jackson … William Jackson.

Even worse was the look in the eyes of Dana Jackson at the first realization that her babies would not be going home with her. That look would haunt Shayna's nights, drive her days. She hadn't yet found a way to erase it from her memory, because if the only way to fade the picture were to see so many that they blend and blur together, then she would rather suffer the vivid few. If there were another way, she would find it eventually.

"Shay, look at me. Look at me, Shay." The singsong sweetness of the four-year-old voice lifted her attention from her book. "Look at me, I'm the badad," he said, a comical sight in the doorway dressed in his father's white shirt with the tail and sleeves dragging the floor. Grateful that this time he was putting clothes on instead of taking them off, she laughed her forgiveness of his third interruption.

"Shay?" A voice still coming from the doorway. "Shay, it's Jean. I knocked and called from the door. When you didn't answer, I

73

thought you must be in the shower, so I let myself in. I hope you don't mind."

"No, it's fine." Shayna rubbed her hands over her face trying to appear more alert.

"What's wrong? Are you all right?"

"I'm fine." She straightened her posture and breathed deeply, then looked up to meet the concern in Jean's eyes. "That's a lie. I'm not fine … I lost the Jackson case."

Stunned, Jean sat down beside her. For as long as they had been friends, she couldn't remember Shayna losing a case. "How?"

"Whatever it was that I needed to do, I didn't do. That's how."

"No. I meant how did he come to that decision? I don't understand."

Shayna shook her head. "There are more than three million households in the United States with children under eighteen that have gay or lesbian parents. All I can ask myself is why not this mother?"

"You're going to be hard on yourself about this, aren't you?"

The fierceness of Shayna's frown surprised Jean. She hadn't meant to make it worse. "You did everything you could, Shayna."

Shayna's tone bordered on anger. "It wasn't good enough. I need to be alone when I'm like this, Jean. Go home. I'll help you move your things tomorrow."

The temptation was to go on home, to leave Shayna to work this out on her own. To leave her as she had found her. But something in Shayna's eyes countered the anger in her voice. A sadness that was enough to convince Jean that she should stay despite Shayna's objection.

Jean remained seated. "You can appeal, right? There's still a chance."

"How many months, or even years, might she have to be without her babies? And if we lose again?" Shayna seemed resigned that Jean wasn't leaving. She locked onto her eyes with compelling intensity. "Have you ever looked into the eyes of a mother who has lost a part of herself?"

Jean shook her head, realizing that Shayna's distress went deeper than a lost custody case. It was personal.

"There's a vast emptiness, a black hole that once you look into it you can't look away. And all the while you can feel an irresistible force sucking the breath from your lungs. Once you've seen it, just remembering it makes your lungs ache." Her voice was soft now, almost a whisper. Her eyes dropped away from Jean's. "I saw it first in my mother's eyes."

Whatever she was about to hear, Jean knew, was going to be painful, both to tell and to hear. She hesitated, then confirmed, "One of her children."

Shayna sank back against the cushions of the couch as if physical comfort would ease the emotional discomfort. "Bennie was number six, after the twins."

Frightening thoughts flooded Jean's mind, and she fought the urge to ask any more questions. This had to be up to Shayna.

"He was so cute," Shayna said with a smile. "Even when I'd have to follow a trail of clothes out of the house and find him naked on the neighbor's swing set. You have to be pretty cute if your eight-year-old sister who'd rather be with her friends thinks so." The smile dissolved quickly, replaced by a pensive stare. "I wasn't a very good big sister."

Things were becoming clearer to Jean, things about Shayna's dedication and her choice of work. No wonder. No damn wonder.

"I wanted to finish reading my book; it was the last chapter." Her stare remained fixed. "*Little Women*. I've never finished it. The baby had a nasty cough, and Mom had taken her to the doctor. Dad and the older boys were cleaning the garage. I was in charge of baths."

Jean sat motionless, waiting. Understanding now what she was about to hear.

Shayna rested her head back and covered her eyes with her hand. Bennie tried to leave the doorway; she fought to keep him there.

"It's okay, Shayna. I understand now."

You don't understand. You can't. It's not what I'm about to say.

It's that I'm finally going to say it. Softly she said, "I have to tell you." She closed her eyes. Benny was still standing there in the doorway, smiling that big-toothed smile, happy and safe. But there was no way she could keep him there, and she couldn't keep trying any longer.

Jean grasped Shayna's hand and held it tightly. "Okay, I'm here."

"I didn't know exactly when the twins finished their baths. I had to read that damn book. Bennie was trying on Dad's clothes and interrupting me, but I kept reading." Tears made their way under Shayna's hand and down to her jaw line.

Shayna, Shayna! Derrick's voice frightened, desperate. Hurry, hurry! He had forgotten to empty the tub and forgotten the boat that had tempted Bennie's reach. The vision Shayna fought so many nights was more vivid than ever.

"He was face down—" Her voice broke. Jean closed her eyes. Tears began to form.

Shayna tried to finish. "Still wearing that big white shirt … Oh, God, he wasn't breathing." Her own long ago screams shrieked in her head. She was grasping at the shirt, at the water, pulling him from the tub and screaming his name. There was confusion and her father and sirens and suddenly arms around her.

Jean's arms held her securely, letting her cry, letting her feel. Letting the woman feel the pain of the little girl she couldn't forgive. Shayna had finally gone to the place she had avoided all those years, where the pain was immeasurable and the guilt unbearable, Jean thought. She was weeping uncontrollably.

The body she so admired for its strength shook weakly in Jean's arms. How can I ease this kind of pain? What can I possibly say? "You were only a child, Shayna. It wasn't your fault." Hopelessly inadequate, she knew, but it was what she believed. How many others have told her the same? How many more will it take?

Shayna lifted her head; wet stains streaked her face. Her words were a whisper. "I knew better."

Jean cupped Shayna's face in her hands and looked directly

into the light brown eyes. "You were a child. You made a child's decision … You have to forgive yourself."

Shayna closed her eyes. "God, I've tried." The tears continued in tracks down her cheeks. "I can't."

Jean pushed back against the couch and pulled Shayna's head against her shoulder. It was the hushed, secretive tone of Shayna's voice that made Jean suddenly realize that not only had Shayna been unable to forgive herself but that she had also been unable to tell anyone about it. It was more painful to watch than Jean had imagined. The woman who was so capable of empowering others was unable to help herself. How terrible it must be to lose someone so close and then to think she must bear the weight of that responsibility forever.

Jean spoke softly against Shayna's forehead. "I know enough about your parents to know that they would never have blamed you. You know that, don't you?" She felt Shayna nod. "They love you unconditionally." I love you unconditionally. "Now you have to start loving you."

Her fingers moved automatically with long soothing strokes over the tiny close-cropped curls over Shayna's ear. Jean would let her cry as long as needed. She would keep her arms around her so that she knew she wasn't alone. The weight of Shayna's body relaxed against her.

"It's okay," Jean whispered. "It's okay." There was nothing more she could do.

Sixteen

Jean made sure she arrived at Shayna's office a few minutes early. It was within her comfort zone to be there before Ken and his attorney arrived, and she wouldn't be pushing those boundaries today.

She passed Shayna's desk and let herself into the small conference room. "Please tell me there've been no surprises," she said as Shayna looked up.

"There have been no surprises. Now sit down and relax." Jean took a deep breath and picked up the papers Shayna had placed at her seat.

"It's not too late, Jean. Are you still sure about this?"

"More than sure. I don't want anything to interfere with the process at this point."

Shayna watched her scrutinizing the first page. "Okay, just checking."

"I thought out this decision carefully," Jean said without looking up. "It wasn't based on toilet seats and toothpaste tubes."

"I wasn't insulting your decision-making process, my friend. You seemed uneasy, that's all."

Jean's head snapped up immediately. "I'm sorry, Shayna. I guess I am uneasy, and totally self-absorbed. I appreciate how well you've handled everything right from the beginning. If it weren't for that, I'd be a lot more than uneasy."

"It has helped that you are both good people still trying to do the right thing."

"Maybe that's part of the problem. I'm trying to hang on to a friendship with him, and I want to know right now whether or not it's possible."

"Only time's going to tell that." Shayna motioned toward the door as Ken and his attorney entered.

The politeness in the room would have been more reassuring if Ken's face had held even a hint of acceptance. He appeared as a shock victim, his reactions out of sync with what was happening around him. Jean avoided eye contact for fear that she would want to rush to the other side of the table, clasp his head to her chest, and promise him that everything would be all right.

When the formalities were over and the papers examined, there was nothing left but to sign at the Xs. Ken rose, papers in hand, and moved around the table to the chair next to Jean.

He gave her no choice but to look into his eyes as he spoke. "I can't believe we're going to do this."

Shayna walked to the other end of the table, but Ken's attorney stayed his ground. Jean found it difficult to ignore him. She took Ken's hand to try to personalize their communication. "I think I'll always love you. But this is something we have to do. We both deserve to be happy."

"And you think this will do it?"

Jean kept her eyes on his despite the tears she saw forming there. She blinked back her own and nodded. "Yes, I do," she said softly.

"I don't think I'll ever be able to say you were right." He looked down at the papers before him. He took a sharp breath and expelled it quickly, then picked up the pen and signed.

When it was over, he followed his attorney from the room without a word. Her composure slipping, Jean turned toward the window.

Shayna waited a respectable minute and then followed and placed her arm around Jean's shoulders. "This was the hardest part, wasn't it?"

Jean nodded and turned into Shayna's embrace. She was so used to being the one that always did the holding and the comforting, making others feel loved and cared for. It felt good to be held. An embrace of simple compassion, no judgments, no conditions.

It had been a long time since anyone had held her this way. Once she had passed early childhood, the comfort of her mother's arms began to include lessons that needed to be learned—God's Word on forgiving those who spread nasty lies about her, the importance of searching out God's plan and not insisting on her own, so many lessons.

The arms of boyfriends had held conditions as well. Sex was the expected proof that their compassion had been effective and appreciated. Even Ken, consoling her after her cat died, had taken the opportunity to suggest that a baby take its place. It always seemed to be as much about their comfort as it was about hers.

Shayna, though, offered only her arms and an unspoken understanding. She was giving what she herself had needed.

Warmth and a sense of well-being, unlike any she could remember, swept over Jean's body. She didn't want to move, didn't want anything to make Shayna take her arms away. She closed her eyes and imagined falling into the deep sleep of innocence before worry and life-altering decisions replace the joys of childhood. She wondered if it was possible for adults ever to sleep that sleep again.

"Are you going to be okay?" Shayna asked. The words were soft enough to be in her dream.

Jean eased from the embrace. "As long as I can keep from thinking about what this is doing to Ken."

"Will you eat tonight if I don't feed you?"

"Probably not."

"Come on, then. We'll feed your body and see what we can do with your spirit."

"Tell me something good," Shayna wisely began.

Jean stopped picking at her food. Her face suddenly brightened. "Yes," she declared, "there is good news. I've been so pre-occupied I forgot to tell you. The school board has decided to keep the Life Fit program intact."

"Ah, yes," Shayna replied with a wide smile. "I knew you could do it. Now that's cause for a smile—" she offered the rim of her glass for a toast "—and a celebration."

Jean met Shayna's glass with her own and smiled for the first time all day.

"What is the most decadent dessert on the menu?" Shayna asked, flipping to the back page.

"Hot fudge brownie delight with whipped cream and a cherry," Jean replied quickly.

"We're having it. And I won't even make you finish your dinner first."

Jean did finish, however, picking away at it through their conversation, her spirit lifting by the moment. It took so little with Shayna. *All these years and I could have allowed myself a friend like this. Someone on the same emotional plane, someone with the same needs, the same goals in life. Could there have been another who would have more evenly shared the difficulties and the joys?* There had been many opportunities to find out—a best friend, a camp counselor, a teammate, a fellow teacher, all willing to share the intimacies of her life. But she had discouraged all their efforts and eventually they all turned away.

Jean looked at Shayna, ordering dessert with that sneaking-candy gleam in her eyes. *Am I as important to her life as she is to mine? Why has it taken me this long to realize it? What was I afraid of, the friendship? Or more than a friendship?* The answer didn't seem important now.

"Would it be terribly insulting to Ken if I took back my maiden name?" Jean asked. "Like I was trying to erase all evidence of that part of my life."

Shayna cocked her head. "Is that why you would do it?"

"If I would have shown that I never intended my marriage to

be permanent, the Church would have annulled it—after all these years, poof, like it never existed."

Jean continued to talk, working through the possibilities on her own.

"Annulment is the only thing my mother would have agreed with—if I was going to refuse to stay with Ken, then at least annul so that I could marry again in the Church … I only married in the church the first time because of her and my dad … I don't want to make this decision because of someone else."

"Changing your name is a personal matter. It should be for the right reasons."

The conversation eased comfortably through Mary Carson's Catholic view of divorce, then shifted to less personal matters. They talked and analyzed and laughed, and made themselves sugar-sick by eating a whole brownie delight each. They were unaware of the time until the wait staff began vacuuming the carpet and placing chairs on the empty tables around them. Like all their evenings together, this one had gone by too quickly.

Large frosted globes shone like rows of full moons along the freshly shoveled walk to Jean's apartment. The air was crisp, the hour was late.

Jean dug her keys out of her bag. "You didn't have to buy my dinner, you know."

"You didn't have to pay my regular fee, either. It's the least I could do."

Once Jean was safely inside the entrance hall, Shayna stopped at the foot of the stairs. But before she could turn to leave, Jean grasped her arm. "Thank you once again for being here when I needed you."

"Just returning the favor. I know how lonely the middle of the night can be. If you want company or just a voice at the other end of the phone, call me, okay?"

"That's a lot to ask from even a good friend."

"Not really." Shayna smiled and tipped her head to the side.

"I have no life, remember?" Her smile dissolved. "But you're an important part of what I do have." She leaned forward and touched her lips carefully to Jean's.

Jean closed her eyes for only a second, while the soft warm touch of Shayna's lips shocked her body with unexpected heat—not the gradual, radiant heat that she had grown to expect from their closeness, but a sudden, intense heat that sparked her whole body. That moment of brief, undeniable attraction brought with it the realization that Shayna was in love with her, and in the next moment, the feeling that it had always been, that she had always known.

Shayna made no further eye contact, and offered only a quiet good-night as she left.

Seventeen

Jean sipped her coffee slowly while a handful of teachers shop talked around her. Larry Tomely, freshman math, claimed the seat across the table.

"How's it going?" he asked, slurping from his cup of get-me-through-the-morning and tilting back in his chair in a manner not allowed by the students.

"Good," Jean answered. She had already concluded that all such questions now included interest in her personal life. They were all aware of her divorce and, to a person, their concern seemed to stem from curiosity. Funny, she thought, how those who had rarely gone out of their way to speak at length, now made the effort. She and her life had become suddenly interesting. Evidently, happily married people were boring.

"I can't believe they're wasting a whole day on career orientation," Larry complained. "Half a day would have been plenty if they hadn't offered such asinine choices. Women in politics, now there's a viable career. I'll bet Ellerton's pissed as hell that he left the choices up to the committee."

Since Jean was the only other one at the table, she felt obliged to respond. "Maybe if one of those choices heads one kid in the right direction it will be worth it."

"For one kid, I'm wasting a whole day of instructional time?

That's a bigger waste of time than art or PE," he said with a sarcastic grin.

Comments that rude would ordinarily get the confrontation they deserved. Not even Brian, with comments she knew were made in jest, could escape a challenge. Today, though, there would be no confrontation. His words and his insinuations weren't enough to change this buoyancy she felt into the kind of mood needed for an effective argument. No, the only battle she would enjoy today would be to pass this chance on to Shayna and watch her sit Larry upright in his chair and erase that annoying smirk from his face. Poor man wouldn't stand a chance, but he'd be arrogant enough to try. Just the thought of it was enough satisfaction for Jean. She checked her watch and let it drop.

"Larry," another male teacher called from across the room. "You coming Saturday?"

"Wouldn't miss it."

"It'll be a good time," came the reply. "There'll be a band and the whole nine."

Larry directed his attention to Jean. "Hey, if you're not doing anything Saturday night, you should go to this party with me."

Arrogant son-of-a-biteh. Insult me, then ask me out. She wouldn't speak for all men, but this one was definitely from another planet. "Thanks," she returned with her most tactful turndown. Nine yards is not a first down. "I don't think I'm ready for that yet."

Jean caught a glimpse of her reflection in the big chrome coffee maker at the end of the table. Well, no wonder, she thought, marveling at the smile on her face. How long has that silly thing been there? Ol' Larry must think it's for him. Foolish man.

"The sooner you get out there, the better," he said as he stood. "Believe me, I know. Well, think about it."

She attempted a polite-only smile. He left with a wink. Not in a million years, Larry. Not interested in spending time with you, or getting to know you. Not interested in sparring with you, or laughing with you, or having a relationship of any kind with you. Teaching in the same building is as close as you'll ever get.

How quickly things change. Within days, women were looking to match her up. Men, like stray dogs sensing a bitch in heat, appeared from nowhere. Conversations no longer centered on teaching; instead they all converged at an uncomfortable personal level. And since she refused to satisfy their curiosities, she found herself spending less time in their presence and more time alone.

The alone time, too, was beginning to test her. She couldn't shake Shayna from her thoughts. She was there day and night, making her think about the next time she would see her, making her consider the questions that continued shuffling through her thoughts. How long had Shayna loved her? When had she guessed her secret? How long would she wait?

When Moni was her student, she hadn't been the first with a crush on her, and Lindy wouldn't be the last. Though schoolgirl crushes seemed insignificant in the larger scheme of things, they had become an unavoidable sojourn to her youth. It was in the eyes of these young girls that the secret was unveiled. Like tiny mirrors, they reflected the truth until Jean could no longer deny it.

Today, in the clear blue of Lindy Dae's eyes, she saw the choices she'd made in her own life.

Lindy sat slightly round-shouldered, tugging periodically at the form-fitting sweater that hugged the waistband of a short blue skirt.

"Pretty sweater," Jean noted. "Is it new?"

"I went shopping with my brother's girlfriend. She was right. I've gotten some compliments today." She squirmed and straightened her skirt. "I hate how I feel in this, though."

How well I understand. The words of Jean's father, long forgotten, came back clearly. "Honey, your mom would have me excommunicated if I let you wear that shirt to church. Run up and change into the one with the lace on the collar, it makes you look so pretty." Scratchy, uncomfortable, acceptable.

"Don't wear it then, Lindy."

"I don't want to look like a lesbian anymore."

"And you gave up your manager's position with the basketball team for the same reason?" Jean attempted eye contact, but Lindy refused. "Lindy, what others think isn't as important as what you think. Do you think you're a lesbian?"

The same question had haunted Jean since her best friend had asked it all those years ago. "Do you think we're lesbians?" Her own answer had been to make sure no female friendships had ever become that close again … until Shayna. Like Lindy, she had run.

She watched Lindy struggling with eye contact, and wished she had the freedom to convince her to be herself. Or at least that she had the power to whisk her past the consequences of denial. Knowing what needs to be done and not being allowed to do it is worse than not knowing.

"I like being around the girls on the basketball team. Maybe I do like it too much … I don't know." Her eyes finally met Jean's. "But if I am, I don't want anyone to know … especially my parents. I never want to hurt them like that."

"The one thing that would break your mom and dad's hearts would be for you to lie with another woman." At the time those words were spoken, in the aftermath of the love letter, disappointing her parents would have broken Jean's heart. It hadn't seemed like a choice then, any more than it did for this girl now. Once Lindy figured out how to make it her secret, how long could she keep it? Would it take her a lifetime to realize that in doing so she would be sacrificing her own happiness?

Eighteen

Jean rose from the pew at the back of the church. She walked the center aisle toward the front, her hand trailing over the ornate carvings at the end of each pew. She had already decided that going there again would not alter her view of Catholicism or encourage a confessional or a Sunday morning visit.

She was there to think through her thoughts in the sanctuary of Saint John's Church, before the statues and symbols of the religion she'd walked away from—the religion that taught a woman to be subordinate to a man, that declared propagation to be the sole purpose of sex, and that proclaimed marriage and children to be the ultimate goal in this life, after salvation and the worship of God. Jean had been unable to accept any of this, even after intensive catechetical instruction.

Has it been twelve years? Discounting the formality of my wedding day—yes, it had been that long since I knelt in this place. That long since communion, and confession. The rebellion during her college years was when she first recognized the hypocrisy of confession and repeated sin. Walking away had been easy then. Those were the years when she was truly free, answering to family only on holidays, exercising tolerance and acceptance of other beliefs and other lifestyles. But in truth, her rebellion had been short and not so extensive as she had once thought.

Sure, she had chastised herself for lying about her true feelings for another woman, declared herself free of guilt, but she had not returned to the camp where she counseled. She had chosen physical education and made friends with a number of lesbians, but she had filled most of her social time with Ken. She claimed proof of what little effect the Church had over her, but married Ken to prove normalcy.

She had broken free, only to begin walking a tightrope, the thin line between truth and acceptance. And she had walked the tightrope so long that it had begun to feel normal. That is, until she met Shayna Bradley, stood solidly on the platform, and realized how good it felt not to struggle for balance.

The church was still, void of music and memorized chants, a vast empty space stretching upward the full height to its ceiling. Nothing to muffle her own small voice, nothing to stop it from echoing its freedom into the majesty of the rafters. Nothing except herself.

She no longer believed that shouting her secret out loud would result in the immediate wrath of God raining down upon her, yet it just didn't seem right to do it here. Revealing it quietly to herself in God's house would be good enough.

What she believed in her heart was that the basic principles of Christianity—the Ten Commandments, the Golden Rule, the omnipotence of God and of Love—were principles worthy of our acceptance. She had even gone so far as to accept the Church's doctrine that the burden of sin must have its source of redemption; for the human spirit is unquestionably vulnerable to error. But, if God exists as the Church proclaims, offers his redemption through the blood of Christ, then what concern should I have for what mortals think? What family members or church members or anyone believes to be sinful in my life is irrelevant. That is between God and me. Yet, others—administrators, school-board members— would judge more severely than my mother ever could if they knew my secret.

They weren't outwardly apparent, but her sins were many. She had camouflaged them so well over the years that it had taken long looks in the harshest mirrors before Jean herself had recognized them. Among them were the lies—the ones to parents and friends and Ken, and the ones to herself. Envy, too, had to be counted. She had coveted the happiness of others and blamed them for the injustice she felt. The hardest to face, however, was what she had done to kill the dreams of another in order to satisfy her own needs. Divorce had been her start at redemption. Someday, when Ken's life wasn't so disrupted, when someone else had eased his self-doubt, she'd complete her redemption and confess to him what she had finally accepted in herself.

What she was not willing to count as a sin was Shayna's kiss. Without guilt, she'd been able to accept it as a gesture of thankfulness for a cherished friendship, a gesture of caring about the state of the other's heart, a gesture of love. The one thing that she might finally be sure of was that love is not a sin.

How long she'd been in love with Shayna, she couldn't say for sure. It had been a gradual process. Love had grown one caring minute at a time. Sharing and laughter and day-by-day conversations had strengthened it. She felt the love before she knew it, and accepted it as she would the regularity of a heart-beat or the necessity of breathing.

Christ loomed before her, hanging limply from a golden cross, awaiting resurrection. If she believed in the spirit eternal and believed in the omniscience of God, then she also believed that Christ knew what was in her heart. There was no need for a priest to hear in a confessional what God already knew.

He knew about the fire that swept through her body when her lips had touched Shayna's. He knew the fierceness of her desire to be held again in Shayna's arms. He knew how desperately she wanted to be a permanent part of Shayna's days, to share her nights. He knew all of this and more.

Nineteen

Piles of clothes filled every inch of the bed. Dresser drawers hung open and half filled, and the closet remained a gaping hole in the wall. Jean looked from one to the other, then with a groan dropped onto the heap on the bed. She stared motionless at the ceiling, wishing that she had started in here instead of organizing her desk in the spare room. The temptation was to fall asleep and worry about it tomorrow.

Twenty minutes later, the ringing of the phone jarred her from a light sleep.

"How about leaving the rest of that mess until tomorrow?" Shayna suggested on the other end.

"I've already come to that conclusion. What do you have in mind?"

"Getting out of here for a while. Let me surprise you. Can you be ready in fifteen minutes?"

"Jeans and a sweatshirt?"

"Perfect. And a warm jacket."

The meteorologists had predicted a hard winter. Signs from Mother Nature had validated their prediction early on. Squirrels, fat and furry by Halloween, had competed with the deer to glean every kernel of corn from the stalks left in the fields. Woolly caterpillars had been thick and plentiful.

It was already the coldest Michigan December in twenty-five years, with record-setting potential as temperatures made a week's run at the zero mark. A sparse covering of snow, offering little insulation against the wind and harsh temperatures and coupling with the results of a dry summer, meant serious danger of dehydration for plants and trees.

Gus and Annie's ancient oak, however, would not suffer. Hour-long soakings from a hose every day of the summer and fall had given it ample water deep in the ground for the roots to draw from all winter long. It stood sound and stable and equal to a unique task.

Shayna stopped the car on the side of the frozen gravel road. As requested, Jean had kept her eyes covered for the better part of a mile.

"Can I look yet?"

"No, not yet. One more minute." Shayna hurried around the car to open Jean's door. She helped her out and walked her through a gate. "Now."

Jean opened her eyes to an astonishing sight, a mystical setting worthy of the Magic Kingdom. Hardly recognizable until she lifted her eyes beyond the lights was a giant old tree, its trunk surrounded in ice that had formed frozen caverns dripping from its lower limbs.

They stood silently through a complete sequence of changing color until the freeform sculpture sparkled once again from blue to purple. "It's magnificent," Jean finally uttered. "But how?"

"Come on," Shayna said, with a childlike excitement in her voice. "I'll show you."

As they walked closer, the depth and thickness of the caverns and their massive stalactite formations became even more impressive. Jean was amazed. "You can walk in there."

"Sure, and if it weren't so late, Gus and Annie would be waiting with hot cider and homemade cookies when we came out."

Jean looked around in the darkness surrounding them.

"How did you find this?"

"Careful how you step; remember, you're walking on ice."

Shayna followed Jean, ducking into the largest opening. "I was driving through the country a few years ago, thinking through a nasty case, and I saw the sky changing colors ahead of me. I followed the roads as it got brighter and brighter until I found this."

They wound through a tight passage illuminated now in brilliant yellow. "My first thought, after being blown away by its beauty, was for the protection of its creator. In law language, this is an attractive nuisance. I was worried about someone getting hurt in here and suing old Gus for everything he had."

"What did you call it?"

"An attractive nuisance. Similar to a swimming pool, something that entices people to investigate where they could be injured. The insurance won't cover any injuries unless the property owner takes prudent safety precautions."

They squeezed between two thin cycles as they changed from orange to red and slid on their feet down a tiny ice slope. "It took a lot of talking, but I finally convinced him to put the lights on a timer so that they go out at ten o'clock when they go to bed. It almost broke his heart to put that fence up. He's been doing this for thirty years without incident, but it scares the piss out of me."

Jean smiled and shook her head. "An attorney who expends that much energy to prevent a lawsuit ..."

"I can't have Gus getting sued. I'd have no frozen fantasy to surprise you with tonight."

"It's far more than that," Jean waited for Shayna's eyes and held her gaze. "And I know it." She broke eye contact and looked ahead into the cavern, now sparkling in blue-green. "How in the world does he do this?"

"Here, come here."

Shayna took Jean's hand and directed her to an opening in the outside wall of ice. She knelt and pointed to a hose nozzle just beyond the frozen flow, directed up into the tree. "There are four of them—" she ducked away from the ice drips "—they run all the time, day and night so that the water doesn't freeze in the hose. The shapes change from day to day and week to week. You never know how it's going to freeze. Every year, it's different. Some years, you can walk all the way around, some you can't."

The excitement in Shayna's voice was endearing. Jean kept her hand and continued around the tree.

"You can walk all the way through this year," Shayna said. Jean was surrounded by frozen water, breathing air that turned her warm breath instantly into visible molecules, yet her face was flushed and hot, and heat radiated up from their clasped hands to warm her whole body.

The feeling didn't surprise her, she had known for years what it meant. It had been there, in varying degrees, whenever her favorite teacher made special time for her, and when in seventh grade her coach had tended to her badly sprained ankle. It had been there when her closest girlfriend had snuggled tightly against her after a scary movie during a sleepover. It was the same feeling from which she had distanced herself after her best girlfriend in high school had shared intimate thoughts and sealed them with a kiss. This time, though, she wouldn't be running.

The opening where they had entered was in view. Jean crouched through a low arch of ice changing from purple to red and stopped. She turned to face Shayna as she cleared the arch. "Why did you bring me here?"

Looking surprised, Shayna replied, "Because it's beautiful, and I wanted to share it with you."

"Why me?"

Shayna hesitated before answering. "Why not you?"

"Indeed," Jean said softly, watching the light turn the sparkles in Shayna's eyes from red to orange and cast a warm tint over her face. Jean stepped close. "Why not me?"

She pressed her lips to Shayna's, full and clear in intent, expecting her kiss to be returned. When it wasn't, she retreated quickly. "I'm sorry, Shayna. I misinterpreted your feelings."

"No, you didn't. You surprised me with yours."

Jean looked puzzled. "I assumed ... I guess I've shared everything except those thoughts with you."

Shayna raised her eyebrows and nodded.

"But, I was assuming ... if a man and a woman spent the amount of time and shared the things together that we have, how would you see that relationship?"

"I might think they were dating, but—"

"What makes what we've been doing any different?"

It was rare for Shayna to be at a loss for words. Jean fought the urge to smile.

Shayna looked down and opened her hands as if it would help the words to form. "Because we ... we've never—" She looked up without finishing.

"Never acknowledged what we were doing? Never put it into words. Have you ever wanted to?"

"Jean, you were married to a man. I thought you saw me as a close friend."

"Have you ever wanted to?"

"Many times. I've wanted to touch your face." She did now, her fingertips glancing across Jean's forehead and down her cheek. "I've wanted to tell you how much I always want to be able to look at it. I've wanted to lift your hair from your collar—" her fingers dipped under tresses yellow-gold from the changing light "—and feel the silk of it falling over my hand. I wanted to find a way to hold you in my life, even if it meant never touching you, never telling you how I feel about you. Whenever the thought of being with you entered my mind, I questioned whether I would know how to be in a relationship with you, whether I would know how to give you what you need."

"All you have to do is love me."

"If it is that easy, you're going to be in my life forever."

Moonbeams of light peered sheepishly through bedroom blinds and whispered over smooth, muscled limbs to tell the secret Jean had kept for years. Her hand sought out the smoothness that she had waited a lifetime to touch.

"I never allowed myself to touch a woman," Jean said softly. "I never could until now."

Shayna whispered into the silk-like hair above Jean's ear. "Maybe it's the right time in your life."

"It's the right person in my life," she said as a sense of well-being followed the course of warmth through her body. "Definitely the right person."

It was her time now to enjoy all that she had denied herself—the gifts of the women who would have been, could have been, lovers, now pouring from the heart of Shayna Bradley.

Jean closed her eyes and allowed tender lips to linger over her lids and her cheeks and the sensitive places along her neck, until they found their way to her own. There they pressed and parted and softened, offering their incredible warmth, until they won her submission. Until she joined the heated search and offered her tongue in return for the growing heat deep in her abdomen.

Shayna cradled the length of Jean's body against her. She expected the sensations of desire, but she didn't expect the overwhelming feeling of love—never before this strong, never before mixed with passion. She held Jean close, whispered the words from her heart. "I love you, sweet woman, more than I can tell you."

Jean's kisses had become more insistent, moving fervently into the hollow of Shayna's neck. "Show me," she breathed. "I need you to show me."

Yes, oh yes, with every breath and every whisper. Shayna would show her with her hands and her lips, with the heat of her passion. She would show her the love that she'd never shown another. Show her now, and for the rest of her life.

Jean's body was flushed with growing excitement, her skin sensitive to the feel of Shayna's body against her, the breasts molded around her own, the smooth muscular thigh sliding between her legs and bringing sensations more vibrant than she could remember. She stretched over the cool sheets and gave Shayna's hands the freedom of her body—willed them from her breasts, pliant beneath them, to the length of her thighs, and back again to her breasts.

Shayna's lips whispered once more against Jean's mouth, telling her of want and need and love, and pulling the breath from her lungs in sighs and murmurs. And hands, with no mercy for her lack of breath, were coming again and again to all the sensitive places, caressing with exquisite tenderness, reaching just this side of every limit.

"Shayna, oh, Shayna … I've waited."

"Yes, yes," Shayna answered hotly against Jean's throat. "For me."

Jean clasped Shayna's head to her chest. The scent of softened curls, sweet with rosemary and citrus and exotic flowers, joined whirling, swirling senses spiraling toward ecstasy. Fingers steeped in the heat of desire electrified her, opened wet velvet, hot and melting, to a pleasure paralyzing, consuming.

Jean gasped her words. "Oh, God." Her body trembled and arched and reached. "I can't … can't … wait …"

The next moment, Shayna's lips were kissing the inside of her thighs, and then her mouth was slow and soft and perfect and brought brilliance beyond pleasure. It filled her with a powerful tension. Breath and brilliance held—suspended, trembling, waiting for ecstasy. And then it came, with a low rapturous sound, gathering and rising and bursting forth in orgasm.

Breathless and still glowing with sensation, Jean collapsed into Shayna's arms. "Such love … such beautiful love."

Shayna caressed the moist skin and pushed dark blond strands of damp hair from Jean's face. "What a beautiful woman you are," she said softly. "So many times I've wanted to tell you."

"How very lucky I am," Jean said, "to have you this close. To hold you and touch you. To finally be able to show you …"

"You have. In so many ways you already have."

"Not like I've imagined. Not like this." Jean brought her

mouth, open and intent, to Shayna's, gave her hands permission to explore and excite, and began fulfilling more than her own promise.

Twenty

The secretary nodded permission for Jean to enter Principal Ellerton's office. The memo directing her to see him had sounded urgent. She slipped it into her attendance book and closed the door behind her.

The room was warmer than the outside office, a whole lot warmer than the gym, and smelled faintly of blended tobacco and aftershave. Chad Ellerton replaced the phone on a desk far too neat to be useful and motioned toward an empty chair.

"Thank you, Jean. I do appreciate a prompt woman." Not promptness, or a prompt teacher. A prompt woman. Did he not appreciate prompt men? Or did he assume men to be prompt and women not to be? Jean smiled politely. Why do I let him bother me so?

"I'll try not to take up much of your lunch period here. I know how you teachers cherish your lunch time."

Do you? Ever taught on your feet from eight to twelve-thirty, answering the same five questions three thousand times, and not having five minutes in which you can get a drink or go to the bathroom? Remember boot camp?

"Cherish is probably a good choice of words. It's rare when students or parents acknowledge the sacrifice that we're making when they call on us during lunch. But—" she smiled again politely "—we do whatever it takes."

"Right, right." He nodded. "In this case, about ten minutes of your time." He cleared his throat. "I'm going to be asking for some assurances from you."

"Regarding what?"

Another clearing of his throat. "I understand that you've been sacrificing some of that cherished time for one student in particular."

"Lindy Dae."

"Yes, Lindy Dae. In need of counseling and advice if she's ever going to fit in, that's evident."

A poorly disguised if-she-walks-like-a-duck assumption. Would he be more concerned about the harassment she's facing if he thought she was being wrongly judged?

"… obviously encourages a certain amount of teasing from other students," he was saying.

Teasing. Oh, that's it, of course. It's merely teasing, not harassment. Nothing out of the ordinary, nothing as drastic as sexual harassment.

"I'm sure you realize how it could look to others when we have qualified counselors in-house, and the student instead is encouraged to spend her time in your office."

Jean held the beginning of anger. "It would look to me like the student isn't comfortable talking with the counselors and sought out someone she is comfortable with. Maybe you're not aware that I have my masters in counseling."

He began with a condescending chuckle. "Well, your position here is still that of a teacher, and unless I want parents screaming in one ear and the school-board riding the other, I can't have my teachers advising students on matters like sexuality, especially you." He looked her straight in the eyes.

Jean felt suddenly short of breath, as if her body was making preparation for a major athletic event, a championship match. She began picking at the cuticle around her thumbnails.

He continued. "There's too much talk out there that will make people wonder why this student feels more comfortable talking with you. You see where I'm going here?"

102

God, like an enlisted man on his first furlough. Despite the sudden realization that she was the subject of far more talk than she had imagined, Jean kept a tight focus on his face. His reddened cheeks and glassy glare sent a painful twinge to the pit of her stomach. If she didn't get out of there soon, her thumbs would be raw and bleeding. *Dare I ask what talk? Be forced to the defense, expected to admit or deny? Tempt the same fate as Dan Sanders?*

She finally found her voice. "I've been careful not to advise anyone on their sexuality."

He cocked his head as if questioning whether she got it.

Exasperated, she asked, "What are you asking me to do?"

"Refer this student, or any student, who approaches you for advice that goes beyond your classroom, to the counselors."

"And if they don't go?"

"That's not your problem. The counselors can make recommendations to the social worker, and we can handle things through the correct channels. That's what they're there for."

Jean finally dropped her eyes and nodded. "Did you know that we had a student kill himself two years ago?"

"One of the secretaries mentioned it."

"An A and B student, a nice kid. The same age as Lindy. He was an assistant in my team sports class." Jean focused on the polished walnut penholder in front of her. "I still wonder what signs I missed. Had he asked for help and I didn't see it or take the time?"

"If there were indications of a problem, I'm sure someone would have referred him."

But maybe there were no indications, other than an unsubstantiated feeling that the boy was hiding his sexuality. Maybe he didn't think he could tell his secret to counselors who had entered the field twenty years ago? Maybe he thought they were out of touch with the needs of their students, ill equipped, or forbidden to deal with problems of sexuality and sexual harassment.

"He obviously didn't feel comfortable enough to ask for help, or maybe he didn't get the right help. We don't know what drove him to the point of taking his own life, but we do know that Lindy is being sexually harassed every day. We're required now by law to take whatever measures necessary to protect her."

His cheeks flushed again. "Don't quote the law to me. You're not talking to some uninformed parent."

"But there are organizations—"

He stood abruptly. "Your job is to teach your classes—mine is to run this school. I expect no more or no less. You're excused, Ms. Kesh."

Jean reached the door in an instant of anger and humiliation. Before soundly shutting the door, she returned, "Please remember that my legal name now is Ms. Carson."

The walk to the gym wasn't long enough to stem her anger. She had only a few minutes to put it aside so that it had no bearing on the way she dealt with her afternoon classes. Trying to teach in an ice-cold gym wasn't going to help matters.

She entered the gym, though, to a pleasant surprise. The problem that they had suffered with all day yesterday and this morning had been remedied. She could no longer see her breath when she exhaled. Jean removed the sign from the door instructing her students to bring jackets and not to change for class.

The advice she had received during her student teaching days and adhered to faithfully had paid off. On the first day she stepped foot in the school, she had wandered about the obscure parts of the building until she had found him. In the dim, dirty corner of the furnace room, sitting at a small table and smoking a cigarette, was the head of maintenance. She had accepted a cup of coffee in an unused, but questionable plastic foam cup, sat in an old folding chair he had hand-dusted, and made her first friend. As a result, her memos were always acknowledged on the day they were received and projects and repairs involving the gym always got done in a timely fashion.

"Hey good-lookin'." Brian's voice echoed across the empty gym. "Do I get my kiss now?"

She furrowed her brow before turning to be greeted by Brian's beaming face.

"Heat," he said, spreading his bare arms in the warmed air. "I got you heat. Isn't that worth a kiss?"

"It's worth my heartfelt thanks if you really had anything to do with getting this place out of the deep freeze."

"Sure I did. Of course you had a little to do with it, too," he admitted. "Remember asking maintenance if a school's heating system has filters like a house?" Jean nodded. "Well, they thought they'd replaced all the filters, but you still had no heat. So, you see that big duct up there?" He pointed toward the ceiling by the south wall. "I got to thinking that, with the wood shop on the other side of that wall, we were probably sharing the same ducts. I got up on the ladder in the shop and, sure enough, there were filters up there blocked solid with sawdust. We replaced 'em and voilà, heat. Go ahead—" he pointed to his lips "—plant one right here."

"You want people to talk?" she asked, with no intention of obliging.

"Aw, they do anyway."

He was the one person who she knew had one ear on the students and the other on the staff; she would have asked him eventually. "Who does?"

He scrunched one side of his face. "Oh, the meatheads in shop talk a lot of trash. I have to set 'em straight now and then."

"Trash," she said with the just-tell-me look that signaled a low level of patience.

"Remember that these guys sit on their brains all day, and the lack of oxygen has caused severe damage." He got the smile he was after, then hit her with the bad news. "They figure you have to be a lesbian because you left your ol' man and you get on them so bad for teasin' Lindy Dae."

Jean stared at him for a second, then closed her eyes and shook her head slowly. "Wonderful," she muttered.

"Don't worry, babe. I'd never let 'em trash my favorite girl."

"Woman," she corrected. "I'm almost afraid to ask what you told them."

"I told 'em I oughta know if I'm having an affair with a lesbian or not."

"Oh," she said, dropping her hands to her sides in exasperation. "Please tell me you're kidding."

"About the meatheads thinkin' you're a lesbian?" Not the smile he was looking for this time. "Somebody has to defend your honor."

"Some defense. Anyone else talking trash?"

"The bitches are buzzin'. But what's new?"

Nothing really. I should've expected that the lounge gossip wouldn't stop at my divorce. I am rumor fodder until something juicier comes along. And being present in the lounge every day won't stop them; it'll only make the mill more challenging to run. "I guess the buzz doesn't bother me so much as who might actually listen. There are teachers who socialize with school-board members, and board members who socialize with Ellerton. I've already been warned not to counsel Lindy Dae."

His tone became empathetic. "You've been under a lot of stress lately. You have to find some way to blow 'em off ... a good movie, a good drunk." He shrugged his shoulders. "When I get to the point where I can't blow 'em off any longer, I figure it's time to do something else. Life's too short."

Some clichés have way too much truth to them. Jean sighed and offered a weak smile. "But that's where we are very different. I don't want to do anything else. I think I'll always want to teach. I don't know what I'd do if an administrator called me in and said they no longer wanted me teaching their children."

"That's not going to happen."

"They fired Dan Sanders."

Brian's attention shifted to the first rush of students entering the far end of the gym. "Yeah, but remember," he said as he left, "he is gay."

Twenty-one

Jean held her tongue as the stack of ungraded tests slipped from her grip and cascaded to the floor in front of the main office. She groaned and knelt to begin gathering the papers. She slid her fingernails under the edges of the bottommost sheets, grateful for a relatively clean floor, and attempted to pick up the pile. But the spread was too wide and the top of the pile slid even farther. With an inaudible mutter, she began again.

The voices coming from the open office door didn't warrant her attention until her name was mentioned. Jean listened closely as she continued gathering papers.

"I've always thought she was, even when she was married."

"Her poor husband—ex-husband—now he's the one I feel for. Do you know him?"

"No, but don't you think he had to have known?"

The need to know who was speaking overcame the sick feeling in her stomach. Jean stood and, without straightening the jumbled stack of tests, she rounded the corner into the office. At the sight of her, two women teachers offered abrupt greetings and expressions that clearly said, Oh, I'm so glad you didn't walk in ten seconds ago. At that moment, Jean realized that it didn't matter who they were. They weren't friends; they were colleagues. What mattered most was that the talk was extensive.

Proof that what she had felt over the past two weeks whenever she entered the teacher's lounge was true. Faces with placating smiles turned her way and conversations dissolved. This was the cross she bore each day in order to stay out of her office during lunch and avoid seeing Lindy.

The teachers whisked past her and left the office, and the secretaries refocused on their paper work. Wishing that she could have thought of a quick, clever response of some kind, Jean turned for an automatic check of her mail slot. The sick feeling in her stomach turned into a flare of anger at the sight of a familiar sealed envelope. "Enough," she declared aloud. "It's enough." She grabbed the envelope and stuffed it unopened into her roll book and hurried out of the office.

Every day there had been an official memo with a cc to her personal file, every day another ridiculous complaint.

Monday: "I observed you chewing gum in the hallway on Friday. One of your own rules states that your students are not to chew gum. You are expected to set a better example."

Tuesday: "All teachers are expected to provide full and adequate lesson plans. Merely noting 'warm-up exercises' at the top of your daily lesson is not adequate. Please list each exercise every day and explain to me how each benefits your students."

Wednesday: "I understand that you participate in competition against your students on a regular basis. This practice is unnecessary and unsafe. I am instructing you to no longer engage in such activity."

Ellerton had sent memos every day for the past two weeks. He was making his point. It wasn't about this one student. It was about any further challenge. It was personal. Ignoring such administrative requests, regardless of their validity, would be considered insubordination—easier to document and prove than incompetence or immorality. The paper trail had begun. She felt anxious and suspicious, even to the point of suspecting Brian of relaying information to the administration.

Yet, of the crosses she was being forced to bear, seeing the look in Lindy's eyes as she passed her in the hall, and knowing that she had nowhere else to turn, was the least tolerable. It touched all the sensitive fibers of her heart and made them hurt.

Teachers have always done more than teach, at least the good ones have. Learning is affected by so many variables, and any or all of those variables that can be identified must be addressed if each child is to have the same opportunity to learn and grow. If the student is bored, the teacher must challenge. If the student is confused, the teacher must clarify. If the student is frightened or worried, the teacher must calm and reassure. The teacher must transform low self-esteem into self-confidence. Every good teacher in every classroom does it every day. Yet when one of the variables has anything to do with sexuality, the teacher must repress seeing and hearing and feeling. It is no longer her place.

Jean picked at her tuna salad while Shayna busied herself in un-familiar cupboards looking for the makings of a walnut cinnamon coffeecake. I should have made an elaborate dinner and been a better hostess for Shayna's first over-night in the apartment. It was no excuse that it was already clear which of them was the better cook.

"I'm sorry, Shayna. I should have had something more ready. Ken was right about my letting my job affect my personal life. I bring it all home."

"Sometimes that's the only place we can find resolution. And cooking is not a problem; it's therapy for me. Talking is therapy for you—so talk."

"There's not much more to say about it. I'm frustrated and worried."

"Worried about rumors and memos, and frustrated about not being about to help a student?" Shayna continued gathering ingredients. "I would expect that of any dedicated teacher. Bowls?" Jean pointed to a lower cupboard. "As far as helping Lindy goes, I could get her an order of protection."

"She doesn't even want the counselor talking with her harassers anymore. She's convinced it only makes the situation worse. And she has stopped telling her parents to keep them from coming in again. I don't know how I'd talk her into something that drastic."

"Sometimes drastic is what it takes. Taking control, letting them know you're serious. But if she won't do it … Had you thought about anonymously bringing in PFLAG or GLSEN to do a seminar? Or the tolerance organization? Have them do an assembly or something on diversity?"

"I dare not be involved with the tolerance group. After a clear warning and all the memos, something like that would definitely be interpreted as insubordination. And I don't know that it could be done anonymously, unless I can find a parent I trust that would be willing to approach Ellerton."

"Mixer?" Jean pointed to another lower cupboard. "How about Lindy's parents?"

"I don't know them well enough. Besides, Lindy is already worried sick about hurting them. I wouldn't want anything to look like we've already decided that she's a lesbian when she isn't ready to make that conclusion herself. Besides, if her parents ever found out that I'm a lesbian, it would look like I'm trying to influence their child's decision."

"How about another teacher?"

"Maybe Brian. I'd have to think about it."

"Uh-uh, you should. I can't find vanilla. Do you have any?"

Jean retrieved it from a box on the counter that had been over-looked in the unpacking process.

Shayna thanked her with a quick kiss on the cheek. "As for your worrying about rumors," she continued, "if you're a lesbian and want to continue teaching where you are, then you have no choice but to comply with protocol. Someone else will have to pick up the torch."

"And if a rumor gets as far as the school board and I'm called to defend myself anyway?"

"If a board member ever asks you if you're a lesbian straight out, you'll just have to lie."

"I've spent most of my life lying. I finally get right with myself, and I still have to lie? Besides, it's not just a matter of my sexuality. Don't you see how easy it is to establish a paper trail that can be grounds for dismissal?"

"What are your alternatives?" Shayna stopped folding the batter and looked across the room at Jean.

The phone rang before she could reply. Jean hurried to the other room. "Ms. Carson," she answered. "Yes, this is she." She walked back into the kitchen purposely to make eye contact with Shayna. "Yes. Hello, Mrs. Dae … No, that's all right. I just finished dinner."

Jean sat back down at the table and listened intently. She is concerned about her daughter and has every right to be. If Lindy were mine, I'd be making this call too. I'd be telling the only person my child trusts how much she has changed, how worried I am, how desperate for help I've become. And I'd expect help.

"Yes, I know Lindy has wanted to talk with me … No, it isn't only that I've been busy. I've been told by the administration that I am not qualified to advise Lindy. Mr. Ellerton wants her to talk with the counselor." The resulting silence was nearly unbearable. "Mrs. Dae, this is breaking my heart. I care a lot about Lindy, and I wish I could help, but I've really been given no choice. Do you think there is any possibility that Lindy would talk with a private psychologist?"

Jean looked to Shayna for confirmation that she would recommend one. Shayna raised her eyebrows in approval and nodded. But Mrs. Dae's response was less than encouraging. "Why don't you talk with Lindy and see how she feels about it, and I'll have someone call you next week … That's okay. I'm sorry that I can't be of more help … Yes, she is. She is a good girl … Good night, Mrs. Dae."

Jean clicked the phone dead and sat silently staring at it. Shayna sat down in the chair next to her and reached for her hand.

"What did I just do?"

"Tried to ease your conscience a bit," Shayna replied. "That's all."

"I don't think it's going to relieve much of anything."

Shayna squeezed her hand. "What would you be doing if your hands weren't tied?"

"All the things you've suggested, plus anything else I could think of to make Lindy's struggle easier for her to live through. And if all else failed, I'd make sure her parents understood Lindy's rights under the new legislation. I don't dare do that."

"The school district has no choice there. It's the law."

"They'll force a challenge in court. This board has a horrible track record. They've disregarded the law on pregnancy leave, and on equal pay for their women coaches. They're just arrogant enough to risk losing another case in court. I guess their thinking is that they'll get away with whatever suits them until they are forced to comply. Ellerton doesn't want to rock his canoe, so he's probably counting on the fact that most parents won't want to put their child through a court case."

"Would it make you feel better to update your resumé and see what's out there?"

"Tuck my tail and run?" Jean dropped her eyes and stared at the plate of half-eaten tuna salad. "But I'm a good teacher."

"Yes, you are. And I'm right beside you whatever you decide."

Twenty-two

It had been almost a week since the last incident. The middle of her locker door—a haze of light red from the cleaning fluid—was still clear of magic marker graffiti. Regardless, Lindy pushed the toe of her shoe into the bottom of her locker as soon as she opened the door to prevent it from being slammed shut over and over. There'd been no recent shoving or books pulled from her arms. She had chanced coming to her locker three times today, and no one seemed to notice.

Lindy checked peripherally right and then left before turning from her locker. She smiled to herself and slid into the flow of students passing between classes.

Jay Markus fell in beside her. "What's up, Lindy?"

Her smile disappeared. She looked straight ahead. "Nothing," she replied quietly.

"You're lookin' good," he continued, brushing against her arm. "Is that a new sweater?"

Lindy nodded. His attention over the week, although a welcomed change, puzzled and worried her. Jay's comments had never reached the cruelty of the others and he had never touched her, but she questioned this turn toward kindness. Maybe Mom called the school again and this time made things better. Had he been threatened with suspension? Had his parents found out?

But why not just ignore me? Is it possible that he's really giving me a chance?

"Bacchaus isn't here today," he said. "We got Miss Wannabe, that sub that always tries to follow the lesson plans."

They reached the intersection, and Lindy turned right toward the biology room. Jay reached out and touched her arm to stop her. "Hey, cut out with us," he suggested. "Breeze and Janelle are meeting me behind the maintenance shed."

Maybe it's a test to see if I'll turn him in. Or maybe he's setting me up to turn me in. She had only seconds to make up her mind.

"Come on," he urged. "Ol' Wannabe's in the hall."

Lindy turned instantly and followed him down the opposite hall. He signaled her to go into the girls' restroom. "Stay in there till I come and get you."

She was sure that she'd made a mistake, sure she was being set up for something. She tried to decide what to do. The restroom was at the end of a secondary hall near the gym, and not widely used. Lindy looked under the row of stalls. She was alone. She took a deep breath and tried to stop her heart from racing. She could just go to class and tell the sub that she had been sick.

"Hey." Jay's voice preceded him. "Come on, let's go."

He draped his letter jacket over her shoulders as they slipped out the side door. They ran down the edge of the parking lot next to the gym, where there were no windows for anyone to spot them. At the end of the lot, they squeezed through an opening in the chain-link fence and cut across the bus compound to the maintenance shed. Breeze and Janelle were already there, settled on upended milk crates and sharing a cigarette. They seemed mildly surprised to see her, but smiled as they offered Lindy an empty crate.

She wanted to make the situation as comfortable as she could as fast as she could. There was only one thing she knew to talk about with them. "I'm sorry about regionals," she said, letting her backpack slide to the ground. "I thought for sure you'd go all the way this year. You played so well, and triple overtime—God! I lost my voice yelling."

Janelle exhaled and stubbed out the butt in the snow.

"Yeah, we would've beat 'em if somebody wouldn't have fouled out." She gave Breeze a shove that almost toppled her from her seat.

"They'd been fouling me all game," Breeze complained, "and I barely clip her elbow on a steal. Hey, it might've helped to have a manager that knew what she was doing. How come you quit on us?"

Jay made eye contact with Breeze, then focused on Lindy. "Yeah, why'd you quit?"

Lindy dropped her eyes, then fished some gum from her backpack. "I was falling behind in a couple of classes." She offered the gum around. "My folks made me quit."

"No-o-o," Breeze exclaimed. "I'd like to see my parents try to make me quit. I'd live someplace else before that would happen."

"So, you gonna come to the team party over break?" Janelle asked.

"I thought you already had it at the end of the season."

"Coach always throws that one, you know, for parents and supporters," Janelle explained. "We're inviting you to the real party at my house."

Lindy brightened. "I'll have to, ah, sure, I can be there. It'll be great. I've really missed everybody."

Breeze offered her a high-five. "All right!"

Twenty-three

"Bundle up. Warm clothes," Shayna directed from the cell phone. "I'm picking you up in ten minutes."

"Where are we going?" Jean was becoming used to the spontaneity, but not every caper needed to be a surprise.

"When was the last time you went sledding?"

"Shayna, it's eight o'clock. It's dark."

"They leave the lights on at the Cascades hill until late. I borrowed sleds from my nephews. I'll give you the fastest one."

"You do know that you're years of therapy away."

"But you love me anyway."

The snowfall over the past two days was finally respectable enough to live up to Michigan's Winter Wonderland nickname. Bright virgin snow powdered trees and rooftops and lay in fresh clean blankets over lawns and streets and cars. The bright lights of the Cascades reflected off the vast white slopes and lightened the sky over the outskirts of the city.

Shayna parked the car and unloaded the sleds, and she and Jean began the trek up the backside of the slopes. Many parents, grateful for the opportunity to get their kids out of the house, allowed them to enjoy the hill later than usual.

"I hope I don't see any of my kids," Jean muttered as they reached the top.

"They'd most likely be snowboarding on the ski slope. Don't worry."

"I feel silly."

"You look adorable," Shayna said with a smile.

The cold night air slashed at their cheeks and made their eyes water as they raced down the hill over and over again. Jean's initial reservations disappeared halfway down their first run. Each consecutive run put the worries of the day farther behind her. Before she realized it, she was laughing and red-cheeked and challenging Shayna to yet another race, unaware that the slopes were nearly deserted.

They raced side by side down the less traveled edge, surprised by unseen bumps that knocked the air from their lungs, and glided to a stop into the snow-bank alongside the road.

Exhausted, Jean rolled from her sled and landed on her back in the snow. "I can't do it. I can't walk up that hill one more time."

Shayna dropped down beside her. "I forced myself to do this last one because I didn't want to be the first to quit."

Jean laughed herself into a giggle. "I was doing the same thing."

Shayna collapsed on her back. "I don't think I can walk to the car."

Jean laughed lightly at the impossibility. "Well, I'm not carrying you."

The snow crunched and stuck to Shayna's hair as she turned her head to face Jean. "You're so beautiful when you do that."

"When I do what?"

"Smile like that. Like you haven't a care in the world."

"I think you have brain freeze."

Shayna removed her glove and wiped the melting snow from Jean's face. "You don't do it enough, you know. You force me to resort to crazy capers like this to enjoy the beauty of it." And cause me to revisit places long abandoned in childhood. Places that once gave me such joy—until Bennie died.

Sledding and skating until our faces were too numb to feel the mucus running from our noses. Huddling together around the wood stove in the warming shed until our fingers and toes tingled again with feeling, then rushing back out to get in as much as possible before Dad picked us up.

Carefree days with worries no greater than getting the chores done in time to watch our favorite television show, and keeping the most precious things on shelves high enough to keep the little ones from getting their hands on them. Do we ever know that we're that happy at the time?

Jean's voice broke her thoughts. "What are you thinking about?"

The instant before she could answer, the huge stadium-like lights turned off, and they lay looking into a clear black sky dotted with thousands of bright stars. Their bodies began to cool with the lack of activity, but Shayna's breath was warm against Jean's cheek. At the first touch of her lips, Jean jumped.

"Relax, honey," Shayna whispered. "It's dark. Barely enough reflection from a new moon to find our way back to the car."

She tried. Jean wrapped her arms around Shayna and tried to enjoy the warmth of her lips. She wanted so badly to add this to her list of firsts. To allow her body to tingle with the excitement right out here in the open without walls to hide her. To enjoy Shayna's love without guilt, without fear. She clung tightly around her waist, while Shayna nuzzled her neck and kissed her face, until something indefinable overwhelmed her. She began to tremble uncontrollably. Tears appeared without warning. Their saltiness alerted Shayna.

"It's okay, baby." Shayna caressed the silky hair, wet with snow, and kissed the top of Jean's head. "It's okay. I thought we had put it behind you for a while. We'll go home."

Jean's arms held their position around Shayna's waist, her face burrowed into the shoulder of her jacket. Excitement and joy, however, shrank rapidly from their embrace. She was power-less to enjoy it and powerless to leave it. Is this the same doubt that questioned Shayna's commitment? The same doubt that kept her from sharing her new relationship with anyone, even good friends?

The words were muffled into the collar of Shayna's jacket. "I'm beginning to doubt myself. Maybe I am wrong, maybe I go too far."

"No, it's not you. Don't let them scare you."

"They do scare me. I don't know what to do. I need you to hold me. Hold me tight."

Shayna gathered her tighter and felt her shiver.

The tears stopped. "I have to feel close to you—very, very close ..." She wiped the wetness from her cheeks on the soft wool of Shayna's jacket. "But I don't think I can make love—not tonight."

"We don't have to make love, honey. I'll just hold you and you can talk to me. Or you can go to sleep, or just think quietly if you want."

"But don't go home after and leave me alone tonight."

"Of course I won't. I love you, Jean. I'll stay with you as long as you want me to." She lifted Jean's face upward to look into her eyes. "If only I had the power, I'd do whatever it took to make it all right for you."

"It isn't your responsibility. No one else has that power. It's someplace in me, but I can't find it."

Twenty-four

They burst through the entrance door and spilled into the hall-way of building G—bundles of laughter and bags of Christmas gifts covered in snow. Still giggling, Jean dropped her bundles to the floor and stamped the snow from her boots.

"You're insane," Jean said as Shayna let the rest of the packages slip to the floor. "Certifiably insane. It's bad enough for me to wait with my small family, but you, waiting until the day before Christmas to shop for your family—"

Shayna clapped gloved hands together and offered a wide smile. "I knew exactly what I was looking for."

Jean stuffed her gloves into the pockets of her coat and placed warm palms over Shayna's cold, wet cheeks. "I think you always know what you're looking for."

Cool, glossy lips met Shayna's as she wrapped her arms around Jean's waist. "I can warm those up for you," she said with a lift of her eyebrow.

"Look into my eyes," Jean directed, "and tell me what you see."

"Mm, let's see." Jean's arms cradled themselves around her neck. "I see joy in a sparkling blue sea, and love directed right at me and making me warm." She squinted for a closer look. "I see a lace doily melting off my head."

Jean laughed and brushed the snow from Shayna's hair. "I

am very happy." Now warming lips pressed themselves to Shayna's, moved against them until they separated into warm wetness. A stirring, deepening kiss, expressing her love and promising more. Happy and free for the first time in my life. Free enough finally to kiss you, to enjoy you spontaneously, right here in the hall like any other normal couple. Nothing could feel better than this.

"Jean? Jean!" The familiar sound of her name echoed down the stairway and startled them apart.

"Oh, God," Jean gasped. "It's my mother."

She grabbed the bags from the floor and loaded Shayna's arms. "Take these up and wait for me."

With surprising swiftness, Mary Carson moved down the stairs. She edged around Shayna, carefully avoiding contact with the packages and her arms, but looked directly at Shayna's face as she passed.

Her tone was hushed. "That was a woman, wasn't it, Jean?" She stared into her daughter's eyes and read her silence. "How can you do this?"

"Where's your car, Mom? I didn't see it."

"We didn't raise you this way. You were raised in the Church. You know—"

"Do you really want to have this discussion here?" She motioned to the hallway lined with doors. "I don't think you want the world to know our business."

The indication that her daughter was about to tell her something she didn't want to hear was enough to send her hurrying out the door.

Jean followed close behind. She had always made it easy on her mother, rarely talking back, walking away from frustration and anger. But, today her mother had invaded her life, and this time it wasn't going to be easy for her.

"I've tried to tell you, Mother, many times, even as a teenager. You wouldn't hear me out."

"And I still won't." Mary stopped abruptly at the door of a plain blue Pontiac.

A loaner. No wonder I didn't see it. "Yes, you will. This time you will." Jean leaned against the door of the car. "You will hear me because I have to say it, and for no other reason." She looked straight into her mother's eyes. "I'm a lesbian. I've always been a lesbian. All the lecturing and catechism and confessing in the world aren't going to change that."

"You're wrong."

Any delusion that her mother would give up easily was gone. Jean tried to focus, ready an answer for a quote from Leviticus or Romans because it was coming up, it always did.

"That is not who you are. What you are doing is the sin. You can change that. If you hadn't stopped going to church—"

"And listening to how everyone else would have me live my life."

"You don't have to listen to anyone except the Lord. The Pope has told us that God demands us to give up our sins. You know the Bible, you know how harshly he deals with those who don't." Her voice was gaining strength and conviction. She was about to take control once again. "He destroyed an entire city because of people like that."

But this time Jean would not allow it. "Like me, you mean. Abhorred by God, an abomination. Commanded by God in Leviticus to follow His statutes or be cut off from my people. Am I an abomination to you, Mother? Would the world be a better place without this sinner?"

Mary's face flushed. She had clearly lost her grip on her daughter's life. "Don't talk to me like that."

"They're not my words—"

"It's the sin, it's that woman that's making you like this. Why can't you see that? Why can't you see what you're doing to yourself?"

"To you. Isn't that what you really mean? Can't I see what I'm doing to you? To my family? To those hypocrites in the Church who pick and choose which statutes to live by, then judge me for doing the same? What parts of Leviticus do you ignore,

Mother? Eating unclean meat? Burnt offerings? When was the last time the Church put an adulterer to death?"

Tears filled Mary's eyes. "You are not the daughter I raised, or you would know how much this has hurt me." She pressed quivering lips into a thin, firm line and reached for the door handle. No lecture, no scripture, no pleading.

"I'm not trying to hurt you, Mother. I'm trying not to hurt myself anymore." Jean stayed her position against the door for a second or two longer. Long enough to feel a control she had never had, but not long enough to savor it.

"Don't worry, I won't spoil Christmas for you. I'll be there tomorrow so that you won't have to explain why I'm not."

"Don't you dare say a word of this to your father," she managed as she squeezed behind the wheel. "It would kill him."

Shayna's thoughts became more unsettling as she waited.

Will this be enough to send Jean running from our relationship? If I were Jean, would I be able to find the strength to live a life contrary to everything I had known? Where would the strength come from? How would I access it?

"I am sorry, Jean." Shayna watched her slink into the chair opposite her. "I should have made sure we were more careful."

Jean shook her head. "I would have avoided it forever. It's done now."

"But it's a hell of a Christmas present. She'll be all upset tomorrow, and your father."

"She won't tell him. That much I know. And I doubt that anything else will change. She'll go to church and light candles and pray for me, and protect him from the horrible secret. She'll go to her grave preserving the image he loves. His daughters will always be his princesses. It's been that way all my life." He never knew about the questionable friends or the love letter from a fellow camp counselor, or my sister's extra-marital affair. And he won't know about this.

"The invitation still stands if you can stand being knee-deep in kids and dogs and their respective toys. You would be welcomed as part of the family. Which means that you would get no special guest treatment, partly because it just isn't possible. But I guarantee that you will leave feeling loved and accepted."

"Thank you, honey. It's actually very tempting," she said with a weak smile. "But in her religiously controlled confusion, my mother would be terribly hurt if I wasn't there. I would be turning her disappointment and anxiety into an even more painful situation. My sisters and their families will be there, and I need to be there and let her keep the family illusion intact. I guess that's the least I can do."

Twenty-five

Lindy stepped out of the blue skirt and tossed it on the pile of already rejected choices on her bed. "Jeans," she mumbled. "I'm sure they'll all be wearing jeans."

She fished through the pile until she found the pair Brandy had picked out for her. A brother in college with a well-dressed girlfriend had its advantages. She donned again the sweater that had received the most compliments, that was the most uncomfortable of the lot, and pulled on the jeans. They were tighter around the waist and hips than the boys' jeans she used to wear.

It was beginning to make sense to her now, this fashion stuff. The more uncomfortable the clothes, the more appealing they were to others. How many times had she heard her mother say, "The things we women do for you men"? She was beginning to understand what she meant, but she still hated it. What sacrifices of comfort do the guys make? she wondered.

"There," she finally decided. "Janelle would wear something like this."

John Dae stomped the snow from his boots at the side door and hung his jacket on its usual peg. "Isn't she ready yet?" he directed toward his wife. "I've had the car warming up for twenty minutes now. It's a good thing I filled the tank up first."

"She's so excited and so nervous." Marlene Dae placed the last of the dishes in the dishwasher and dried her hands. "This is what it should be like—watching and waiting and worrying," she said with a smile.

"I'll never understand why it takes you women so long to get ready to go somewhere."

"She wants to look just right. You guys only appreciate the end result." Her eyes held a hint of coyness that wasn't lost on her husband. "I'll go see if I can help."

He thought he saw a lightness in her step that he hadn't noticed in years. It made him smile. "It's snowing," he called after her. "Tell her I said to be careful driving."

A large country yard covered in cumulative layers of snow absorbed much of the music and laughter coming from the century-old, two-story house. Light glared from every first-floor window, and cars filled the long driveway. Christmas was over, but the holiday break and Janelle's party were in full swing.

There were no geeks or freaks or goths or skaters there, only jocks and friends of jocks. Lindy, after spending the first hour expecting to have to ignore the usual name-calling and innuendoes, was surprised to find none of it. At the least, she was left alone to help herself to a variety of snacks and sit in on a basketball conversation. Even her worst harassers seemed unbothered when she joined the group watching their air-hockey games. She rooted for Jay, but he lost.

He scratched his name at the bottom of the challenge sheet. "No way," he said, pointing at the winner, "that I'm losin' twice." His Schwarzenegger accent was barely recognizable in his low "I'll be back," but Lindy smiled anyway.

He disappeared into the kitchen and minutes later returned with two beers. "A brew for my girl," he said, offering the bottle to Lindy with a friendly smile.

Her heartbeat quickened immediately, and her face flushed. She left the warm one she had been nursing since she arrived on the floor and sipped from the cold one. "Thanks." His girl. She looked around quickly to see that others had heard him say it. It made her feel strangely giddy. She decided right then that her acceptance lately was definitely linked to Jay.

She stayed close by him. He clowned and joked; she laughed. She cheered him on in air hockey, he won. They danced in the big room where the boys' hands were beginning to fondle their partners and the girls were rubbing against the bulge in their boyfriend's pants. Some of them disappeared upstairs.

Someone handed her another beer. Despite her promise to her parents, she drank this one. The party began to liven even more. Most of the boys and some of the girls took a dare and stripped to their underwear, sat in the sauna until they were red and dripping with sweat, then ran yelling out into the snow to make snow angels. It was funny, those who had been stumbling from the effects of the alcohol now seemed more animated in the snow.

The less adventuresome or the less intoxicated—she hadn't decided which—stood watching with her from the big front porch while nearly naked boys and girls laughed and wrestled in the snow. Lindy watched until they all began moving like cartoon characters, one-dimensional, one mechanical speed. Their voices, too, changed. She wondered where they had gotten the helium.

Weird voices. She frowned at her name. "Lindy, what's up?" All sounding the same. "Come on, come inside." Was it Jay's voice? "You're okay ... just drunk." She closed her eyes, but the voices kept talking in that weird tone. "Aren't you my girl?" Then echoed into the distance. "Chill, man ... chill ... chill ..."

She remembered the laughter and the feel of someone's cold, wet skin. She remembered dizziness and the lack of sensation in her legs and the thought that her mother would be so disappointed. And then she remembered nothing.

Twenty-six

The only light in Jean's bedroom was a blue luminescence cast from the solid color of the television screen. The video had ended unwatched some time ago.

Sometimes worry and stress can so adversely affect a relationship that it drives away the one person whose support one counts on most. And even when it hasn't happened yet, merely the fear of it can add anxiety to the already complex mix of emotions. Maybe a friendship could pass the test of strain, but could the exclusive intimacy of a new relationship stand it? That question was never far from Jean's thoughts.

There were times when she made love because she needed the closeness and she knew Shayna wanted to. There were also times when lovemaking wasn't emotionally possible, when she hoped that Shayna could see that beyond the immediate hurdle, and maybe the next, things would be better. Other times, the passion of new love won out and nothing else mattered. Tonight was one of those times.

Jean closed her eyes and let Shayna take her to a dimension where memos are forgotten and stress is soothed away by the touch of her hands. She gave the sensations free reign of her body, allowed long gentle caresses to increase them here and sustain them there.

Soft lips traveled the planes and covered the contours of her body, coming back often to brush over her eyes and her mouth, whispering of love and beauty. The words quickened her heart. The feel of Shayna's body, naked and warm against her own, brought desire quickly to its pinnacle.

With a moan she reached for Shayna's hand, ready to direct it back to the wetness, desperate for the touch of it to send sensations past the edge of her control. Jean took a sharp breath and pressed upward with her hips, only to be startled still by the loud ring of the telephone.

Shayna lifted her head from Jean's breast. It was one-thirty.

Jean expelled an audible breath at the second ring, disengaged herself from Shayna, and picked up the phone. The message was short and unsettling.

"What is it?" Shayna asked.

"I don't know." Jean sat up quickly. "Someone said that one of my students needs me in the school parking lot."

"You couldn't tell who it was?"

Jean shook her head. "Male, but the voice was muffled."

"Did it sound like a prank?"

Jean gathered her clothes. "It doesn't matter," she answered, hurrying into the bathroom. "I'm not going to take the chance."

Shayna met her at the sink. "We're not going to take that chance."

They were dressed and out the door within ten minutes. In another five, they were making the turn into the first driveway of the high school. The front lot was deserted, but as they rounded the corner to the side lot a lone car was visible parked near the fence.

"Do you recognize that car?" Shayna asked.

"No, I don't know what most of them drive. Can you see anyone in the car?"

"Drive closer with your headlights on it."

"Oh no." The headlights revealed a figure slumped against the steering wheel. "It's Lindy." Jean put the car in park and got out. Passed out? Drunk enough to try to prove that they're all wrong, that she isn't a lesbian? That she can party with the best of them. That she can sleep with boys. And she thought her parents were worried before?

Jean knocked on the window and opened the door, but neither act woke Lindy. "Come on, Lindy, wake up. We have to sober you up before we take you home." She shook her by the shoulder, gently at first, then harder. When there was still no response, she shrieked Shayna's name.

But Shayna was there, already at her side, already checking Lindy's neck for a pulse. She avoided Jean's eyes, knowing that they would only intensify her own fear and magnify her personal struggle. She needed to stay calm, focus, concentrate. "Keep trying to wake her," she ordered.

She walked a few steps away from the car, turned her back, and dialed 911. She took two deep breaths to steady her voice, gave the information needed, and added, "Weak pulse, shallow breathing. Hurry."

Jean seemed to be losing control, shouting demands for Lindy to wake up, shaking her harder. Shayna pulled her away and, despite a clear memory of Bennie's limp weight in her arms, repositioned Lindy against the back of the seat. She straightened her head and tilted it back against the headrest to ensure a clear airway. Again she checked for pulse and breathing. Weak and shallow, no better than before.

Jean had begun to pace, mumbling to herself. Shayna handed her the phone. "She is breathing. I'll watch her while we wait for help. Call the Daes. Try not to alarm them any more than you have to, but find out which hospital they prefer."

For the next ten minutes, Shayna divided her attention between monitoring Lindy's breathing and reassuring Jean, who was becoming increasingly anxious.

"Why aren't they here yet? Shouldn't they be here by now?" Jean paced past the door again, looking toward the entrance of the parking lot.

"Give them two more minutes, then call again."

"I know CPR. I should be helping her."

Shayna took Jean's hand and held it close to Lindy's nose and mouth. Warmth was evident against the coldness of her hand. "I don't think we should assist as long as she's breathing on her own."

"We can't just do nothing." She reached in past Shayna and took Lindy's arm. She rubbed it vigorously. "Come on, Lindy." She was nearly shouting. "Come on. Do you hear me? Wake up."

Shayna understood Jean's anxiousness. "That's good, keep trying to rouse her while I keep track of her pulse." She felt the fear that there was something more that they should be doing, the fear of a life resting on their actions or lack of them. Fear that a decision she felt sure of may actually be wrong.

Shayna could barely feel the faint pulse against her fingertips while her own pulse ran hard from remembered terror. She knew that the only thing that would keep her own panic in check was to keep a steady vigil and to maintain her routine—watching Lindy's unconscious struggle, checking, reassuring, checking again. Yet the whole time she kept her vigil, repeating it, focusing on it, her father's prayers echoed in her memory. "Please, God, not my baby. Please don't take my baby. I'll do whatever you want—" tears running courses down the big man's cheeks "—just give me back my baby."

Tears made their way down Shayna's cheeks. She couldn't stop them, and she couldn't let Jean see them. She kept her head turned toward Lindy, wiping the tears, until she heard the siren in the distance.

The next hour was a confusing mix of emotions and questions and hurried emergency-room procedures. They were left to wait. The four of them—Shayna, Jean, the Daes—occupied the dimly lit waiting room at the end of the corridor.

Mrs. Dae sat in silence; her eyes fixed on the wall of windows glaring with fluorescent light from the hallway.

John Dae, hands in his pant pockets, got up and walked—stopping at the doorway, stopping at the drinking fountain, staring without purpose at the parking lot from the windows at the end of the hall, and stopping at the closed emergency-room doors before returning to the waiting room. Moments later, he would again begin his trek.

Unable to stand the silence and unwilling to start a meaningless conversation, Shayna left the room. She found the coffee machine and began filling cups. There was little else she could do, and it was unexplainably reassuring to sip even a bad cup of coffee.

All Jean had needed to hear was where Lindy had been and her suspicions were automatic. She had always fought the temptation to accept the attitude of teachers like Brian who pigeonholed kids and rarely gave them the opportunity to prove their assumptions wrong. If they were indeed hopeless, then what was her purpose in trying to educate them? Yet at this moment she felt an over-whelming fear that Brian was right. She looked at the worried eyes of Mrs. Dae, still staring through the hall windows, and knew she couldn't be the one to voice those fears.

The pale blue eyes shifted to look directly into Jean's. Marlene Dae looked older than her fifty-seven years; the skin around her eyes sagged, her mouth was thin and tightly drawn. She spoke with a tone Jean imagined would be heard in a confessional. "I read Lindy's journal." She hesitated, as if waiting for a reprimand. "Last year, just before Christmas. I found it accidentally. I was just looking in her closet for a little square box to wrap a present in … I wasn't going to read it. I put it back twice before I did."

"Did you ever tell her that you read it?" Jean asked.

Marlene dropped her eyes and shook her head. "I should have told her that I knew what she was worrying about. I should have told her that I loved her just the way she was, that nothing would ever change that." The soft, pale eyes met Jean's again. "What if I never have that chance again? What if—"

"Sh, no." Jean took Marlene's hand in both of hers. "You'll have that chance. You can tell her as soon as she wakes up. It'll be the first thing you tell her. You have to keep your thoughts positive. She needs our good thoughts right now." She said all the words she knew she should say, none of which she believed.

Shayna returned with the coffee and a reassuring hand on Jean's shoulder. Her legal mind had finally taken over, relieving her emotionally, sorting through scenarios and their possible charges. Did Lindy drink too much on her own? Was she goaded? Forced? Who provided the alcohol? Had someone drugged her?

All thoughts stopped when an emergency-room doctor escorted John Dae back into the waiting room. He dragged a chair across the carpet so that he could sit facing the women. John chose to stand beside his wife's chair.

The doctor's voice was a low monotone. "There's been no change in your daughter's, in Lindy's condition. She remains in a coma."

Mrs. Dae lowered her head and covered her eyes with her hand. John Dae gripped his wife's shoulder.

The doctor continued. "We tested for drugs. As we suspected, the culprit here is GHB. It's odorless and tasteless and, in liquid form, can be easily slipped into the alcohol we found in her system. She probably didn't know."

John asked what Jean already knew. "Is that the date-rape drug?"

"It has been used for that purpose," the doctor replied. "But we don't know any more than what I've told you at this point. What we can assume, from other patients who have reacted similarly to this drug, is that she was probably violently ill at some point before becoming comatose. It no doubt scared the hell out of whoever was there. I can tell you one thing, without that phone call to Ms. Carson, Lindy wouldn't even have the chance she does have."

The breath caught in Jean's throat.

John's question was a plea they all felt. "But we got her here in time, didn't we? She is going to be all right, isn't she?"

"There's no way I can sugarcoat this for you."

A shock of fear hit Jean's chest. She couldn't imagine being in

John and Marlene's place. The thoughts bombarding them must be horrible. The doctor's words were sounding like a fading dream.

"Our experience with cases like this is that it can go either way. She could simply wake up, or she could go deeper into coma and never wake up. There are some neurological tests we can do to determine brain activity, but all we can do is attempt to keep her stable. The rest is up to Lindy. And God."

Marlene buried her tears in her husband's embrace; Jean buried hers in her hands. Shayna sat quickly and wrapped her arm around Jean's back.

"Can we stay with her?" John asked.

"Yes, of course," the doctor replied. "We'll put her in a room where you can stay right with her."

Jean went to Shayna's reluctantly, respecting the Daes' need for privacy and realizing that there was nothing more she could do there. Jean sat on the couch wrapped in a blanket and the comfort of Shayna's arms.

"I can't stop thinking about what Lindy must have been going through, all the time we were …"

Shayna shook her head. "Don't claim that guilt. You couldn't have known what was going to happen."

"Maybe she wouldn't have felt the need to go to that party if I had stepped up to the responsibility and either given or gotten her the help she needed."

"Or if her mother had or a counselor or any number of other people aware of the situation."

"That attitude is exactly how it doesn't get done in the first place. I don't have to stand up; someone else will."

Jean was right, there was no refuting it. What worried Shayna was where this kind of guilt was taking Jean.

"I can't stand this. How could I possibly cope with her death? How could her parents?"

"Jean, you've done everything that you were allowed to do. This is a burden you don't need to bear."

Jean suddenly faced Shayna. "My God. What you must have felt." She cupped Shayna's face with her hand. "What you must still feel. I can only begin to imagine. I thought I could make it better for you by letting you talk about it, by putting my arms around you, by showing you that no one blames you for what happened. But now I see that it's too deep for me to touch, for anyone but you to touch."

"You have helped. Knowing that you know me, with all my flaws and my weaknesses, and that you love me anyway. I never wanted to take that chance with anyone else."

"Isn't it clear now that that isn't the problem, that it never has been. The problem is whether or not you can love you, flaws and all."

Jean kept her eyes on Shayna's. The light brown reflection was clear. "Will I ever be able to love me?"

Twenty-seven

Jean spoke softly to Marlene Dae. "Please go. You and John go have a real dinner tonight, no hospital food. I'll stay with Lindy until you get back."

Marlene looked to her husband.

"She's right," he said. "It'll do us good."

"I'll be right here," Jean assured them. With one look back at Lindy, the Daes left.

Jean took a seat next to the bed and picked up the pale, limp hand. She looked at her own hand in contrast. Long, slender fingers, stronger than they looked, nails French-tipped and meticulously groomed. Mature. Experienced at things that Lindy's have never felt. Long past the first intimate touches, the first exciting sensations that Lindy's may never feel.

She caressed the cool, smooth skin on the back of Lindy's hand with her thumb. "I'm sorry, Lindy," she whispered. "I left you on your own when I knew I shouldn't." Her voice rose above a whisper as she looked at the silent, young face. "Teachers aren't perfect. We sometimes let personal things affect our professional lives. We sometimes make selfish decisions. At the time we don't see the harm in it. It's not that we don't care. We do, we all do—your teachers, your counselor, Coach Porter, the girls on the team. We'd have done things differently if we had known the consequences."

Carefully she stroked Lindy's forehead and touched the tender eyelids. Tears filled Jean's eyes. *If only there is something I can do now, some penance I can pay, that would open these eyes again.* Her voice dropped to a whisper once again. "I was never too busy, Lindy. I was too afraid."

Jean walked the long hospital corridor alone, as she had every day this week. She had asked the same questions of the nurses and had gotten the same answers and had gone home every day to an empty apartment. Then came the questions with no answers.

They weren't easy ones. What decisions could she live with? When did self-fulfillment become selfishness? When did compromise become weakness? And when had truth become a liability? Questions, in the end, that only she could answer.

The excuses she used for not sharing with Shayna this time, so filled with anxiety and fear, were probably valid enough. *There was no need for Shayna to go through this, dredging up bad memories, sacrificing personal time and time away from work. It isn't Shayna's responsibility. Besides, my approach to handling the situation,* she rationalized, *is a mature one.*

In reality, she knew that it was a psychological footrace, very similar to the one she had run at seventeen when she had put distance between herself and the girl who wrote the letter that her mother had found. She could admit this much, that she was once again running from a relationship with a woman. But the stakes this time were much higher. It was more than the condemnation of her parents and the Church and the rejection of friends and family that frightened her. This time she was smack in the middle of an even worse nightmare. Her college years of rebellion had been too little and too late. The Church had done its job. It had imprinted its message on her soul's conscience and had planted the seed of fear.

God's warning in Leviticus had been clear. "And if ye will not yet hearken unto me; then I will punish you seven times more for your sins. And I will break the pride of your power; and I will make your heaven as iron, and your earth as brass." It had taken extensive reading and much thought before coming to a personal belief that the death of Christ offered forgiveness that had not been attainable during the years of the Old Testament. The blood of Christ atoned for the sins of willful humanity.

But what if she was wrong? What if loving Shayna was indeed a sin, and unforgiven? And if unforgiven sin would not go unpunished, then her greatest fear now was that her punishment would not be reserved for the afterlife, but would keep her from teaching and make her responsible for a young girl's death.

How much guilt, how much regret, how much sacrifice would she be asked to live with? Did she have Shayna's strength of spirit, her dedication, to do what it would take to make the changes, to make the part of the world that she could reach accountable? Could she look into the eyes of every student and pledge the full extent of her ability, even if it meant that doing so would mean doing it alone? Which sacrifice, personal or professional, would leave the fewer number of casualties?

One decision, at least, had been made today. Never again would she sit at the bedside or the graveside of another child knowing that she could have done more. Never again would she watch through guilt-shaded tears while another child fought the battle alone. If she was to debate administrative decisions and accept the challenge that could make a difference, then her personal life would have to be beyond reproach. The sacrifice must be a personal one.

It had taken until late in the evening before Jean had the courage to call Shayna. It was actually courage spawned from selfishness so that she could avoid still another sleepless night.

As Jean explained her decision, thoroughly and as calmly as emotions would allow, it occurred to her that she was envious of Serena's ability to talk to Shayna face to face. Serena had had the strength of conviction to overcome emotion, to look into Shayna's eyes and, through tears and doubt, to say the words.

Not that Jean wouldn't face her. She would, and soon.

Their friendship was never in question. She simply needed time to douse the physical flame, to be sure that the next time they were face to face that she wouldn't once more end up in Shayna's arms and in her bed.

Shayna listened to what amounted to a carefully thought-out breakup. Here it is, the point where the weight surpasses the inner strength to carry it. Although she had contemplated its possibility, even feared it, the initial shock of it shook her like a judge's decision going surprisingly against her. All other indications had led her to believe that her logic had been right on target and that her assessment of their relationship true. To be told that she was that wrong was difficult to accept. Still, she listened carefully, her own heart beating with painful anxiety, waiting for a hint of emotion that would tell her that she hadn't been entirely wrong— a break in Jean's voice, a quiver, some indication of what was really in her heart.

In her own heart, the thought of losing Jean's love was causing a pain, the intensity of which had been rivaled only by the loss of Bennie. She couldn't stop it, and she doubted that she could ever make it go away. She was out of her realm, equipped only with skills of logic to argue emotional matters.

"You really think that we can stop this relationship before we're in too deep? How is that possible, Jean? How do you decide what's too deep? How many times we've slept together? Whether we've moved in together or not? What's too deep for you?"

Jean hesitated. "I don't know."

"Well, wherever it is that we are right now, that is too deep for me. Saying good-bye here won't end it for me."

"I'm not saying good-bye, Shayna. I never intended that. Our friendship is one of the most important things in my life."

"There's the problem. You are the most important thing in my life. Case files now sit on my desk where they belong, not in my living room. Time with you even takes precedence over time with my family. Thoughts of you bring me joy during the day and long-

142

ing for you at night. You've rearranged all the priorities in my life."

"But I never expected you to do that for me, and now you're asking me to do the same. I was asked to make that sacrifice before. I couldn't do it then, and I can't do it now."

"And the reason is that you don't have the strength to do it, you don't understand your own power. I'm not asking you to sacrifice your life's work for me. Of all people, I should understand not being able to do that."

"But loving you may mean that I have to. Don't you see that? This is an at-will state. I have no guarantee from system to system, from year to year that I will have a job. This is my chance in life to make a difference."

"Ann Arbor offers protection. The school district just approved a new contract with benefits for same-sex partners. And Ypsilanti has a civil rights ordinance."

"Two cities. We can't all teach in two districts."

"Move with me to a state that does offer you protection."

"Make you leave your practice and your family for me, for a job that's protected for how long? Until the next school board or the next congress decides that I'm no longer worthy of protection?"

Shayna spoke at the end of a long silence. "When I was on the other end of this argument, I didn't understand the full truth of it. Now I see. Love establishes the priorities in your life without thought of sacrifice. It comes down to how important it is to you to keep me in your life. Now I know that it's more than you can give."

"Don't say that. I do love you, Shayna. I don't know what I would do without your friendship."

"You have other friends, Moni, Katherine. Good friends that you've neglected for too long now."

"I need your friendship. We were friends for years before we were lovers."

"And I was in love with you the whole time. I don't think I can do that again."

"Please, don't say—"

"Call Katherine, Jean. I'm not good at good-byes."

Twenty-eight

The sleepless nights didn't stop. Anguish and loneliness and tears filled them. Jean functioned on nutrition bars and coffee and an hour of sleep during her prep period and another at the hospital. How long was God going to make her suffer? How long was the penance for sleeping with a woman? She had done the right thing, made the sacrifice. Things were supposed to get better. Yet nothing was—Lindy, the nights plagued with self-doubt, the questions facing her each day.

"Hey, good-lookin'." Brian reached in front of her to open the gym door.

It was a lie; at least, it was this week. She was so far from good-looking that she was avoiding looking at anything capable of a reflection. Makeup covered the darkness under her eyes but couldn't conceal the puffiness. She was too tired to do anything more than wash and comb her hair. Worse yet, she felt ugly.

"Any change in Lindy's condition?" Brian asked.

Jean shook her head. "They're doing more neurology tests today."

"How are the Daes holding up?"

Better than I am. "Remarkably well. They really believe that their prayers will be answered."

"I take it you're not so sure."

Jean dropped her roll book onto the bleacher and sat down next to it. "I don't even think the questions are going to be answered."

Brian propped one foot on the bottom seat of the bleachers. "So far, none of the kids are talking. There's no doubt; peer pressure is powerful stuff. Have the police found anything?"

"Nothing. The police have questioned everyone at the party. Janelle's parents were out of town for the weekend. Some one cleaned up real good, no trash, no bottles."

Brian straightened and pulled the waist of his jeans back up to its limit just below the excess of his belly and tucked his shirt back in. "Kids are too smart nowadays. Shit, I thought I was a genius when I found someone to buy me beer, and was able to slip past my parents without stumbling or getting close enough for them to smell me."

"I don't know if they're so smart or if it's that stuff is so much more accessible now. Kids have communications networks that we couldn't have imagined."

"Yeah, even fuck-ups come out lookin' like geniuses," he said, swaggering away from the bleachers as the flow of students from the hall burst through the gym doors. He nodded toward them. "Anyone of them could be guilty, and every one of them knows who is responsible. But getting them to talk?" He shook his head.

Since he was the only member of the group she had in class this semester, Jean watched Jay Markus closely. He'd been dressing for class every day even after the end of the badminton unit. She wanted to believe that it was because he saw the benefit in doing so, but she knew it was more likely because this was a basketball unit.

Planning a popular unit immediately following one that was unpopular, especially with the boys, usually guaranteed Jean forgiveness and professional survival. Today, giving the class a choice so that they could play pick-up games was personal survival. She declined all offers to join in and observed from the bleachers. She was much too tired to challenge an administrative order today.

She watched the pickup game at the north end basket. Jay was a lazy jumper, relying on his height to block shots and grab rebounds. But he moved well around the basket offensively. Jean watched him place his hand playfully on the head of a shorter boy whose guarding skills were already ineffective and pass the ball over him. Jay was having fun.

The longer she watched him, the more evident her anger became. He'd been at the party, been a part of what had happened to Lindy, she was sure of it. And yet he could come to school, hang with his friends, eat lunch, and play pickup games as if nothing had happened, as if Lindy's struggle, going on somewhere between this life and the next, had no effect at all on his life.

When during our growing-up years does conscience become fully developed? Does Jay not have a conscience? Or is it not speaking loudly enough? Surely he understood the magnitude of the situation, of owning up to responsibility this crucial. Even if he wasn't directly responsible, or more aptly if someone else was, wouldn't he want to make sure it didn't happen again?

She couldn't pinpoint when her own conscience had found its voice, but she could remember her younger sister waking in the middle of the night at age six, crying and full of remorse for having picked the prettiest gourds from a pile in the neighbor's yard and bringing them home without permission. No one had asked, no one knew. There was only the voice of conscience haunting her sleep until it brought her to tears. What could bring Jay Markus to tears?

She couldn't watch any longer. Relying on years of practice, Jean gathered her anger, wound it like an unruly cord, and stored it away. She waited until the end of the period to avoid unnecessary resentment from Jay, then called him to the bleachers.

"Sit and talk with me for a few minutes, Jay. I'll write you a pass for next period."

He sat without a word, resting the length of his frame back on his elbows.

She would show no anger, neither would she show mercy, for Jay or herself. "It's been a rough couple of weeks. I keep wondering if there was anything I could have done that would have altered the course of things. Maybe Lindy would be here with us instead of lying in a hospital bed." Jean finally looked into Jay's face. He was staring across the empty gymnasium. "Do you think I could have done anything that would've helped?"

He looked at her with a quizzical frown. "No. What could you have done?"

"Whoever gave her that drug didn't value Lindy. They didn't care about her feelings or her welfare. They did something to her, even if they didn't intend it to be this serious, that they wouldn't want done to themselves." He continued his expressionless stare across the room. "Part of my job as a teacher is to instill in my students a sense of respect for each other. Maybe I failed."

Jay remained silent.

"Did you see Lindy at Janelle's party?"

"Yeah, I saw her."

"Do you know anything about what happened?"

"Huh-uh. She was fine when she left."

"She drove herself from the party?"

"Yeah, I guess so."

Jean stared at him until he made eye contact. It might have been something in his voice, or maybe it was in his eyes. "You were the one who called me, weren't you?"

Jay dropped his focus and sat up. "I'm sorry about Lindy, but I didn't call anybody." He stood and stepped down from the bleachers.

"If Lindy makes it, the person who made that call is responsible for saving her life."

He shrugged and turned toward the locker room. "It wasn't me."

148

Twenty-nine

The Bradley house was unusually still, void of the visitors who were usually reserved for weekends and holiday bustle. Shayna couldn't remember a time when it was this quiet.

She let herself in the side door and helped herself to a cold Squirt from the refrigerator. "Anyone home?" she called as she passed through the hall toward a flickering light from the living room.

The man on the television screen was moving his lips to the accompaniment of raspy breathing coming from the other side of the couch. Robert Bradley covered the length of the couch, a sleeping brown bear in green sweats.

Shayna smiled and took the remote control from under her father's hand. He sputtered awake.

"Hey, Papa Bear, how many commercials ago did you mute this thing?"

He cleared his throat and grabbed the back of the couch to pull himself upright. "I must've closed my eyes for a second."

"Or two," Shayna said with a smile. "Where is everyone?"

"Let's see. Tilly's at play practice." He cleared his throat again. "Your mom is sitting with Derrick's brood. The baby has a bad cold, so she thought it would be better to go over there."

Shayna leaned and kissed his cheek. "How are you doing?"

"Great. I cooked myself two Coney dogs with the works and a big plate of cheese fries. Man, that was good."

"Why do you do that?"

"Do what?"

"Tell me these things, then expect that I'm not going to side with Mom and get pissed at you."

Robert chuckled. "One night's not going to kill me. If you had been here two hours ago, you would've been eating one right beside me."

"That's beside the point. My doctor didn't bawl me out like a disobedient child on my last visit."

"I hope you have something more significant than my diet to talk about."

"I do." Shayna clicked off the television and settled into the armchair near the couch. "And unlike you, I actually listen to advice."

He laughed. "Okay, okay. I'm listening. But I'd rather hear that you found the back of the skull in the Jackson case."

"Found it," she said with a nod, "and about to strike on appeal next month."

"The grandfather?"

"Just as I had suspected. It took some searching because he had moved a couple of times, but I found a trail of unprosecuted molestation complaints. And what lit my fuse was a statement from son William after the last complaint that said that he would assure that his father would undergo psychological treatment."

"He knew." Robert shook his head. "And parents, unwilling to put their kids through any further discomfort, settled for just ridding their community of him."

Shayna nodded. "But not this time. A reversal of custody is the least of Mr. Jackson's concerns now."

"That's my girl," he said, clamping the nails of his right hand over the fist of his left.

"That's something I do well, hang on and ride out the toughest battle. It's what makes me effective professionally. But it's no good in my personal life. I don't know when to let go."

"The mongoose hangs on because to let go would mean its demise. It's instinctive. Reason tells us when to let go."

Shayna rested her head against the back of the chair and stared at the blank gray of the unlit ceiling. "And if we still can't?"

"Then something is clouding your thought—" he patted a thick hand over his heart "—emotion, grief or love."

Shayna frowned at the obvious. "But how do you clear it and let go?"

"If I had that answer, I would also have a book on the *Times* best-seller list that was making me big bucks. Realistically, I think it's something that we each have to come to on our own. But maybe if you give me some specifics to work on here."

"Jean walked away from the relationship. I thought maybe if I understood why, I could let go of it. There are so many other things involved for her that I can't accept that she just doesn't love me as deeply as I do her."

"If that were the case, then you think you could accept that it was over?"

She stared blankly for a moment. "I could accept that it wasn't meant to be, but it wouldn't make it hurt any less."

Robert watched his daughter's face. What he saw there made him proud—strength of conviction, honesty, sensitivity. He loved her with all his heart, but he too had had to learn to let go. He couldn't take away her grief, and he couldn't take away her pain. The best he could do was offer his hand as she endured it.

"I want her to have Mom's courage and your perseverance. I want her to trust in her own power and have peace in her heart. But I'm powerless beyond wanting it for her. I can't change society or take away the fear that comes from her religious upbringing." She was reasoning her own release.

Robert listened without intervention.

"I don't have the faith to believe that things will magically work out for the best, for her or for me."

"It's helped give me peace to believe that nothing happens

without purpose. Faith is just trusting that the purpose is there before you can see it."

"Do you ever stop worrying about them?"

Robert shook his head. "Not as long as you love them."

"I'll always love her. She is … was so much a part of my life."

The silence that settled between them was undemanding, unchallenged. Its language was clearer than words.

Some moments later, Shayna said, "I know what the purpose is. I've been looking at it for two weeks, not wanting to see it, wanting it to be more than that."

As tears formed in her eyes, he said nothing.

"I've watched Jean take the guilt for something she couldn't stop." Shayna stopped and looked into the eyes that had always offered her forgiveness, and this time she accepted it. Tears rolled down her cheeks. "Dad, I couldn't stop it either. I loved Bennie, but I'm not responsible for his death."

Robert rose from the couch, placed his hand around her head, and held her firmly against his hip. "No more than Derrick is for not emptying the water, or Daniel for leaving his boat in the tub, or I am for dividing my attention too widely. It took all those things to come together for reasons only God knows."

This time she heard the words, this time she believed them. Shayna wrapped her arms around him and let the little girl she had hated for so long enjoy her father's arms.

"It took years, but I believe we've been shown at least one of God's purposes. A young woman, driven by a passion to give back to the world, put herself in a position to make life better for a lot of women and children. Of that, Bennie's spirit has to be very proud."

Thirty

The alarm clock blared continuously from the bedside stand. Jean lay motionless beneath the comforter, staring at the ceiling. She made no effort to reach the alarm.

Five-forty-five. Six o'clock. Six-ten. The hornlike sound permeated the room. Finally, Jean rolled her head on the pillow to look at the clock. She reached out, dropped her hand on the snooze bar, and left it there. Silence resonated in her head while reason fought for a voice. You have to get up. You have to try. You can't just lie here. Try. Get up and go to work.

She moved slowly, emerging from the covers to sit on the side of the bed. It had never been this difficult. Even with the flu she had always managed to get up; often going to work when she shouldn't have. In ten years, she had called in sick only twice.

Lately, though, she was finding it more and more difficult to function normally. She wasn't sick, not even with a cold, but things that should take little effort and no thought were monumental tasks. Deciding what to wear to work was such a dreaded chore that she avoided it by remaining in the shower until the water ran cold. Her exhaustion went beyond the physical. Psychologically she had dropped to her knees.

Jean looked again at the clock. Today it wasn't possible. She

153

picked up the phone and dialed the office. The automated secretary waited for her message. "This is Jean Carson. I'm ill. I will not be coming in today."

She crawled back under the covers and closed her eyes.

Darkness muted the shapes in the tiny living room. The only light, seeping dimly through the hallway from a slit at the bathroom door, washed into gray over the back of the couch where Jean sat. Until this morning, every day of the past week she had done the same: visit the hospital after school, drive through McDonald's for coffee and a cup of soup, and spend the rest of the night sitting in the dark.

She had tried to reach out. She had called her younger sister and Katherine and even Ken. Their reactions had been predictable. Dig your heels in as you always do, change is vital, make it happen. What else could they say? They knew nothing beyond the events at school. There had been no mention of religion, no confession of sexuality, even to Katherine. And Katherine had been chosen over Moni for good reason; Moni would not only have figured it out, but she also would not have worried about the impoliteness of saying so.

She had kept her relationship with Shayna from everyone, even close friends, even when she knew how much it hurt Shayna. She had rationalized that she wasn't certain that this could be a lasting relationship, that she was unsure if Shayna really wanted the same kind of committed relationship. More truthfully, her subconscious had anticipated the surfacing of the real problem: her own uncertainty.

Now, with tears running down her face, she stared into the most severe mirror of all, the one she had so skillfully avoided most of her life, her own conscience. She was too tired to look away.

Eyes closed, she spiraled through the years, looking into the ever-changing faces that claimed to be Jean Carson, all the way back to the heroic face of a fourteen-year-old Jean. Anger from the homophobic name-calling of her best friend had blustered

154

her cheeks red and sent her racing across the football field in skirt and pantyhose to tackle and pummel the worst offender. Proudly she had worn the muddy hose and tattered sweater as triumphant scars of victory. All the way home, she had sucked in her friend's praises and flipped a mental finger at oppressors everywhere.

But the face grew older and maybe wiser. The college freshman with mentor-like confidence had explained away the letter of expressed love from a fellow camp counselor and dismissed her emotion as displaced admiration.

So sure in the eyes of others, the friend, the heroine, the mentor. She'd spent her life seeing herself through other's eyes, never chancing a look inside, never trusting what she might see.

Through her father's eyes, she was the perfect daughter, thoughtful and kind, proof that good genes produce beautiful children. In her mother's eyes, she saw the blessings of the Father, the wayward child worthy of patience and prayer that would soon bring her back into the fold.

And it was in Amelia Fulkner's eyes that Jean the activist had been born. Far more than Jean's thoughtful analysis of *The Catcher in the Rye* and *To Kill A Mockingbird*, Amelia Fulkner saw in Jean Carson her need to ask why and the perseverance to find how. She saw in Jean the social consciousness and ambition of her own youth. She had challenged her, and questioned her, and praised her, and never once had doubted her assessment of her.

Jean had accepted in varying degrees all the visions of herself. Everyone else's assessments, everyone else's assumptions. It made them happy; it kept her safe. Until what she saw in Ken's eyes pushed her out of her comfort zone. She couldn't be the wife he needed. She couldn't accept his affection while she hid secret desires. She couldn't be the good mother, couldn't narrow her priorities to the raising of her own children. And she couldn't keep letting him think that she could.

Then, for such a brief time, she thought she was exactly as another saw her. Through Shayna's eyes, she was the confidante, the helpmate, the lover, the friend. Giving honestly, receiving graciously. Praying it would last, wanting to believe in its truth.

The spiraling continued, the faces circling and changing, challenging her to decide, demanding acceptance.

She owned them all, each was a part of the progressive self. But where was the power that fused the truth of each into the whole? Who was she through Jean Carson's eyes?

In her semi-sleep state, another voice broke into her thoughts. It was soft and husky, and it whispered to her in the darkness. Shayna was telling her that she had waited for her all this time, was speaking the intimate words and confidences of a lover: "I've allowed myself to believe that you're real." The words swelled in Jean's heart, threatening to burst it open, just as they had the first time Shayna had spoken them.

Jean opened her eyes, but the voice didn't stop. It continued whispering plans for the future. The ring of hope and excitement started her tears all over again.

She had done it again, had destroyed hope in the heart of someone she loved. She reached for a Kleenex from the lamp table, but the tears splattered the letter on her lap before she could catch them. Gently she dabbed the Kleenex over the wet spots before they blurred the handwritten words.

She lifted the paper into the faint light to read again the words she had nearly committed to memory.

Jean,

My feelings for you go beyond what I am able to express in words. I have no delusions of this letter being able to change the effects of a whole life full of experiences. I know firsthand how improbable that would be. Whatever changes occur in our lives will occur from within; our only limitations are the ones we put on ourselves.

I know how important teaching is to you. I know how much you care, how much you want to do. And I know how afraid you are of it all being taken away. But, I don't think you know

156

how much power and courage you hold deep inside. You can be so much more, Jean, do so much more.

I have watched women terrified of losing their children tap into a power and courage that they never realized they had, because for them their children's well-being was paramount. It rose above personal comfort, it negated the very fear that forced them to take a stand. And they stood, strong and uncompromising, and by doing so they showed their children the most important lesson in life. Stand strong for what you believe to be right and true, and the risk will never be too high.

You can teach that lesson, Jean. Right now I know that you think the risk is too great, that not being able to teach would be the worst consequence. But maybe you are in place to take that risk and teach a lesson others can't. And maybe there is a path for you beyond teaching, or beyond teaching here, a step you can't take until you've taken this one. It's a step that will need your very best to take. You would never teach half a lesson to your students, or give them only half of what you could. I know you; you give them the best of your talents, the best of your abilities. Didn't God give you what you have to be used for the greater good? If you withhold that from others aren't you allowing them to be less than they are, less than they can be? Teach that lesson, Jean. Give them your very best. Stand tall and strong, and show them how to do the same. There is no one who can do it better than you.

You will remain in my heart always,
Shayna

The hand with the letter fell heavily to her lap, and her head dropped to the back of the couch. She would let exhaustion carry her into sleep and to a place in Shayna's arms where she would have everything she ever wanted, if only for a little while. Tomorrow she would find the strength to get up.

Thirty-one

The afternoons were growing longer, the sun resting low now in the south-facing windows for only a few hours. Shayna lay stretched across the couch, chest and chin propped over a bunched pillow while the sunlight faded over the pages of her book. She'd read them once long ago and much about the March family had been forgotten, but not their names. Meg, Beth, Amy, and Jo were unforgettable *Little Women*. Each of them had a personality distinctly her own.

Reading as an adult, however, she could appreciate things her child's eyes never caught. She marveled at how simply the author had encapsulated the four personalities on one page merely by having them describe their favorite castles in the sky.

Meg, if she had her wish, would manage a house filled with luxurious things and do it alone without a man. Beth's dream would be to stay safely at home with her parents and help take care of the family, while Amy's would be to travel to Rome to be the best artist in the world.

Shayna's favorite of the little women, though, with her rebellious nature and ambitious dream, was still Jo: "I'd have a stable full of Arabian steeds, rooms piled with books, and I'd write out of a magic ink stand, so that my works should be as famous as Laurie's music. I want to do something splendid before I go to my castle—

something heroic or wonderful, that won't be forgotten after I'm dead."

What grand dreams they had, what idealistic visions of happiness. How stubbornly would they cling to their possibilities? How soon would life temper their hopes, or how soon would one or more of them beat the unrealistic odds to fulfill their childhood fantasies?

For years, the answers may just as well have been locked aboard the *Titanic* for the effort that it would have taken Shayna to find them. An ocean of grief, weighty and vast, had covered the book as if it were a grain of sand, its existence overshadowed and minute. Until now. The reading of it had pushed past the tightening nausea in her stomach and endured the anxious trembling of her heart. Only now was she beginning to realize the importance of finding the answers.

For it wasn't the answers themselves but the process it took to find them that had brought her to this different place. Each page of that last dreaded chapter, left unread for so many years, brought her up through the depths and out of the tendrils.

When she closed the cover of the book, she knew it was all right to have gone back. It needed to be finished, and now she could breathe. She hadn't left Bennie smiling in the doorway or hanging limply in her father's arms or lying in a grave forgotten. He was still in her heart, and it was okay to have moved on. He would always be there, fused to the lining of her soul where nothing could touch him. He was an essential part of her, part of what made her who she was.

Perceptions change. Mansions are just old houses. Monsters under the bed are forgotten socks. Heroines smoke. Unless halted in time by some unnatural force, even castles in the sky change.

It seemed so simple. "When I was a child, I spoke as a child, I understood as a child; but when I became a man, I put away childish things. For now we see in a mirror, dimly, but then face to face. Now I know in part, but then I shall know just as I also am known." The nearly forgotten verse, I

Corinthians 11–12, memorized as a teenager, had held no meaning until now.

It was time for Shayna Bradley to look at herself with adult eyes. She was no longer a selfish little girl. Her castle in the sky—to stand atop the podium as the world's top Iron Woman—had dissolved with Bennie's death. There were no more castles. She had had no right to the attention or the focus on herself. She wasn't worthy of the time and the devotion and the sacrifice necessary for the pursuit of such a dream. A childish, selfish dream. She had given it up after Bennie died.

There had been no room for dreams or castles during the tough times. Her days and nights moved past her on an unstoppable conveyer belt. People and houses and parts of her life moved swiftly by her while her only focus was to keep her footing. It took all of her energy to keep from falling.

But she had kept her footing, and in the process had formed new goals. Her new goals offered a chance for redemption. If she could reach those goals, she could begin to pay on her debt. Through adult eyes, Shayna Bradley could now see herself as she was seen. It was time to claim her own goodness.

Thirty-two

The excitement and commotion of a pep assembly are naturally contagious. Students charged into the gymnasium, excused from classes so that they could stomp their feet to a primal beat and try to out shout each other. The sound of blaring horns and booming drums careened off expansive block walls. Overly spirited cheerleaders bounced and danced and shook blue-and-gold pompoms for basketball players with distinctly higher levels of testosterone than athletic skill.

The frenzied combination rolled and swelled with enthusiasm until the Admiral stepped to the microphone. The noise settled quickly into a steady clapping beat, a demand the Admiral understood. He removed his suit jacket and hung it over the microphone. The chanting grew louder, the clapping got faster. He slipped off his tie and tossed it into the third row of bleachers. The demand continued. The Admiral stooped and slowly rolled up one pant leg past his knee. They weren't satisfied. He began unbuttoning his shirt. The noise became deafening. Teasingly he pulled the tail of his shirt from his pants, slipped the shirt off, twirled it twice over his head, and flung it into a standing throng of students.

Jean watched with the other teachers who lined the entrance wall of the gymnasium. Brian whistled and clapped next to her. She looked down the line of colleagues; most of them were laughing and clapping and caught up in the contagion. None of them, she ventured, would really want to see the Admiral stripped past his T-shirt and pants. But they groaned nonetheless along with the student body when he held up his hands in surrender.

A forgiving energy filled the room, one that pulled together factions that may have had nothing else in common, and focused entirely on something safely universal. It didn't matter who you were, what your parents did for a living, or where you lived, your voice was always welcomed in the bleachers.

Jean had experienced how forgiving it could be firsthand during the girls' season. The Admiral had approved the same number of pep assemblies and had given the girls' team the same special considerations as he would have for the boys', right down to his popular striptease. Only a few short years ago, coaches and parents were demanding that their girls not only be given equal opportunity to play the sport but given the same respect and recognition as well.

Despite her anger toward him—and at times it was barely controllable—Jean found herself appreciating him for the fairness he exhibited toward the girls' programs. She even told him so when he arranged for spectator buses to all the tournament games. No past administrator had ever tried to squeeze the extra money out of the budget. If a student couldn't find their own transportation, they didn't go. The Admiral not only made sure they had a safe, free ride, he made sure the practice began with the girls' season.

Her appreciation, however, hadn't stopped the memos.

They were merely less frequent, showing up in her mailbox at various times of the day and on varying days of the week. They were insurance for him that she not forget who is in charge.

The school song, a catchy marching tune, rang out from the bleachers. The words were simple, the notes reachable. Jean sang along by rote. Her thoughts, though, were on Lindy. She should be there in the bleachers, singing and cheering and sitting with the basketball girls.

"Six-foot-one, junior forward, averaging fourteen points, ten rebounds, and six assists per game, Jay Markus." The name caught Jean's full attention. She'd been watching as the coach introduced his players, and clapping at the right times, but she hadn't really been listening.

Jay ran onto the court with long, loping strides and joined the line of players in their blue-and-gold sweats. High-fives and bravado. He was the knot in the pit of her stomach. She tried to keep from looking at him.

Instead, she looked at the faces in the bleachers, smooth with youth, flushed with naiveté. They were invincible, blow-drying daily tangles free while adults struggle to pull life-as-usual between the teeth of a fine-toothed comb. The change that happens, that takes them from there to here, won't be apparent for years.

She turned to the faces lining the wall. The eight-to-three's were talking among themselves while the coach gave his speech. It occurred to her that those who appeared to be listening, regardless of their differing opinions, were the ones who could effect change. They were the ones who never missed a staff meeting or a union meeting, the ones who listened and voiced their opinions instead of grading papers while others made the decisions. But the issue of sexual harassment hadn't been put before them. Their awareness was as individual as their handling of it. Some had an impact, some didn't. She had spoken to all she dared, but a unified effort seemed impossible. Most weren't willing to say what Ellerton didn't want to hear. And it was hypocritical of her to expect others to do what she was unwilling to do herself. What was it Gandhi said?

The coach was finished, the necessary announcements made. Ellerton had reclaimed the microphone. "Before we leave today," he was saying, "I'd like us all to take a moment to remember that one of our students couldn't be with us today. If you will please, give me a minute of silence for Lindy Dae."

Jean was surprised and infuriated all at once. A minute, a

165

minute of our thoughts. Is that all she's worth? She glared at him standing there like a pillar of righteousness. He's off the hook, the school is off the hook. He thinks they have no responsibility for what happened because it happened off school grounds.

Her strides were swift and sure and headed straight for the middle of the gymnasium and the microphone. She couldn't stand it. Something inside her was erupting, something that had lain dormant for far too long. Gandhi's words came back to her, "You must be the change you wish to see in the world."

You must be the change. The words gained emphasis with every stride. You must be the change. She asked Ellerton politely for a moment to update them on Lindy's condition, and he, in a position of compromise, consented. The irregularity had everyone's attention.

"I'll only take a couple minutes of your time. I know you're excited about the game tonight, but as Mr. Ellerton has asked, it is important for us to remember that Lindy won't be able to be with us tonight. Her family would like me to thank all of you who have come to visit at the hospital, and for all the cards you have sent. They read them to her every day, hoping that she is able to hear them. They know it is important for her to know how much you care."

She scanned the faces, calm and serious now, some looking down, most looking back at her. "I wanted to tell you that her condition is unchanged, except that each day that she remains in a coma lessens her chance of coming out of it. It is a very real possibility that we may lose one of our own, a classmate, a friend, a manager." Except for a few foot shuffles and seating adjustments, the room was attentively silent. "A mother could lose her youngest child, a father his little girl, a brother his baby sister, someone they loved with all their hearts. Not from disease, or illness, or a car accident. Lindy may die because of us."

More uncomfortable shuffling from the bleachers. Jean chanced a look to her left. The lineup against the wall was staring in silence. Ellerton's expression was pulling rank, but he made no move toward the microphone. "Because of you and me, because we were ignorant of how to stop the harassment that she was enduring each day, because we didn't care what was happening as long as it wasn't happening to us, because we were intolerant of anyone who was unlike ourselves."

She hesitated for a moment; not purposely to let her words have time to imprint, but to gather the impetus needed for a soul cleansing. "Or," she added, "most unforgiving of all the reasons, Lindy may die because we were afraid. Afraid that by standing up against something cruel and unjust the spotlight might shine too brightly on our vulnerabilities, our insecurities, our secrets, and announce them to the world. Afraid that we wouldn't be able to tolerate what we expected Lindy to tolerate every day."

Jean stopped and took a deep breath. The humming of the speakers high on the walls and the pounding of her own heart were now the only sounds she could hear. She had one more thing to say. "You know, heroes are not people who planned to one day jump into a swirling river to pull a child to safety. Heroes are people like you and me doing what we know in our hearts is right."

The silence held until Jean reached the door. Then the deep, hollow clap of a man's hands started an applause that swept quickly across the room.

"Hey, sister golden hair." Brian's voice reached her before Jean could get in the car. He stopped his bowlegged swagger at the back of the Ram, two cars down from Jean. "Where can I join your mutiny?"

Her smile was surprisingly comfortable. "Meet me in the unemployment line."

Thirty-three

Selfish woman, is it self-righteousness that puts you at this door, or is it an undeserving faith in the truth of Shayna's love? Jean was unable to answer her own question, and unable to bring her hand to Shayna's door. She couldn't face her when the choice was hers, when her thoughts were inward and bathed in fear. Should this be different, now that she may have sacrificed her right to decide, now that the choice may no longer be hers to make?

Maybe Shayna would not risk going through this again, building her hopes for the future on the love of such a selfish, unreliable woman. Maybe she would hold true to her goodbye. Where would be the reason to risk otherwise?

Jean turned away from the door, unprepared to argue her case. The blame for her loneliness was her own. The irony was that she had finally tapped into a power that had been there all along, but she had done it too late to share with the one she loved.

The fear that this was the last time she would walk this sidewalk followed her. She slowed her steps one last time near the retention pond, where a flock of Canada geese had chosen to spend the winter. She watched them for a moment, a habit she had begun with Shayna early in their friendship. A small pleasure lost now. There were many more pleasures that she would either abandon or learn to appreciate alone. She turned her head and pressed on toward the car.

"Jean."

She turned at the sound of her name.

Shayna pulled the key from the lock and started down the step. "I was digging these boots out of the back of the closet. I'm sorry I didn't hear you knock."

Shayna stood like a champion steed, black boots and jeans and brown bomber jacket. Jean's heart raced, and her thoughts stumbled in adolescent clumsiness.

"It looks like this isn't a good time anyway. You're on your way somewhere."

"It can wait." Shayna stepped toward the door. "Come on, come in."

"Are you sure?" she questioned, but her feet were already trying to catch up to her heart. "I didn't mean to disrupt your plans."

"A phone call will take care of it."

"Not if it's Serena. I've made that woman angry enough at me for one lifetime."

"It's not Serena. I'm going to take my sister through the law library for a paper she's writing." Shayna picked up the phone and dialed before Jean could get her jacket off. "Actually, she preferred to go tomorrow."

She was making this way too easy, accommodating her. Jean dropped her reservations as Shayna dropped the phone. "You didn't hear me knock because I didn't."

"So if I hadn't been leaving just now, if I hadn't caught you, would you have come back?"

"I think eventually. I don't know if I could have stayed away long without knowing."

"Knowing what?"

Jean stepped closer, her eyes fixed on Shayna's. "If you would forgive me. If I would ever have your arms around me again."

The next instant, Shayna wrapped her arms around Jean and held her in an embrace as she spoke. "There's nothing to forgive. That part of your journey had to be traveled alone. I had to understand that. I thought you would want me there, that you needed me there, because you had no one else to go to. I was looking at things in my own shoes, not in yours. I have always had my parents and my family to go to. I have always had their understanding and unconditional love. They've shared my burdens, even the burden of Bennie's death. If they hadn't, I doubt I could have survived it. I couldn't conceive of you bearing and making life-altering decisions alone. I wanted so badly to help you, I wanted us to find the way, but I didn't know how."

Tears formed in Jean's eyes and overflowed. "I love you, Shayna. I don't ever want to be without you."

"The moment I first realized that I loved you was the moment that I felt that same fear, the fear that you might not always be in my life."

Jean lifted her head to look into Shayna's eyes. "I want to be. No matter what else happens, I want to be right here. Please believe that."

Soft lips brushed over the salty wetness of Jean's cheeks. "I do believe that."

"I know I've been selfish."

"But for good—"

Jean touched her fingertips to Shayna's lips. "There was no other way for me to get deep enough inside myself to find out what I had to know. No one else could go there with me."

Shayna nodded, placed a kiss on Jean's forehead, and let her continue.

"I couldn't help anyone else until I learned the lesson life was trying to teach me. I had to leave behind my own burden before I could help lift anyone else's. I learned that lesson too late to help Lindy. But it's not too late to help others. I owe that to Lindy."

"You owe it to yourself. You know it's okay to care about

yourself as much as you care about those kids. In fact, it's essential that you do. You can't give what you don't believe you have. If I had learned that lesson earlier in my life, maybe I would have understood the difference between romantic love and true love before I hurt so many people. Maybe I could have been learning how to love someone else all that time if I had believed in the possibility of you, if I had believed myself worthy."

"You're worthy of so much more than me."

Shayna smiled and caressed the side of Jean's face. "I see we have some work to do on that lesson."

Jean closed her eyes and rested her face in Shayna's hand. "What do you suggest?"

"Something tactile, where you can feel and see and hear just a fraction of what you mean to me." She touched her lips tenderly to Jean's chin and her mouth and the tip of her nose. "We can start there."

Jean's voice was a whisper. "How I've missed your touch."

"Stay with me," Shayna whispered against the tender skin below Jean's ear, "and we'll catch up."

Jean tilted her head submissively while Shayna's lips continued over the graceful curve of her neck and found their way to the little hollow at its base. Warmth followed their trail and radiated downward. Jean spoke with her eyes still closed. "Do you think that's possible?"

"What, honey?"

She could feel her body—warming and giving and feeling wonderful—beginning to relax against the contours of Shayna's. "For us to catch up."

Shayna cradled her affectionately. "Tonight?" she asked, pressing her face into the silky hair above Jean's shoulders. "Absolutely not. If we take our time, it could take a week, or a month, or longer."

Jean's hands moved, refreshing their memory of the firm shape of Shayna's back. They followed the long muscles along her spine as they tapered to her waist and spread over the hard, round buttocks. "I don't think it's possible at all—but I'll stay for as long as you're willing to try."

Thirty-four

Jean stood watching the heaviest snowfall of the season from the glass doors in Shayna's dining room. Summer's toys and joys, covered under nondescript mounds of white, were now only guesses.

"I can't go to the hospital again," she said without turning around.

Shayna placed a plate of warm zucchini bread on the table, then slid her arms around Jean's waist from behind. "I'm not complaining, I just wondered why you hadn't gone."

"The longer she's in this condition, the less likely it is that she'll wake up. Day by day I see the hope slipping from their faces. I see only a pretense of faith now. They've all but given up. But they're afraid not to believe. They won't be able to get to the anger until she's gone."

"Maybe it would help if you'd let me come with you."

No, it would be easier to stay right here, Jean thought, with my eyes closed and my mind in limbo and your arms lovingly around me. We could share a quiet dinner, watch a movie, and eat ice cream for a late dessert. We could have an abnormally normal evening, then make love until we fall asleep in each other's arms. What would I be willing to give for one evening with nothing in it outside of pleasing each other?

"I don't want to be there when—"

"Let me go with you. The Daes are counting on your moral support. We won't have to stay long."

Jean nodded. Her conscience wouldn't allow anything else.

The parking lot had ample spaces available, the elevator was empty. Two young girls sat in the darkened waiting room, watching teenage actors on a sitcom unfamiliar to Jean. It was well past the more popular visiting hours.

The sense of dread that had increased throughout the week slowed Jean's steps as they walked the hallway that tonight seemed unusually long. Please let everything be okay. Don't let it happen tonight. Please not tonight.

They rounded the corner, passed an empty nurses' station, and were partway down the hall when a nurse rushed from a doorway and headed the down the hall the other way.

Jean halted suddenly and grasped Shayna's arm. "It's Lindy's room," she gasped.

An instant later, Jean was running toward the room, her heart pounding in panic. Please God, no … Oh no, please God.

The sound of a woman crying stopped Jean short of the half open door and sent her turning abruptly into Shayna's embrace. "Damn him," she cried into her shoulder. "Damn him. What good were all their prayers?"

Shayna held her, while the sounds of the two women's sorrow tightened her throat. There was nothing she could say. Any talk of purpose or of trying to find the good in tragedy would have to come much later. This was not the time to talk of lessons learned. Now was the time for facing disbelief and for grieving.

Shayna held her until a nurse emerged from the room and recognized Jean. "Please go in," she said with a hand on Jean's shoulder. "The Daes have been asking if you were here."

Jean nodded and looked at Shayna.

"I'll come in with you."

Reverently they entered the room. The first thing they saw was the back of Marlene Dae. She was hunched over the bed and appeared to be clutching her daughter's hand to her breast. Before anything could be said, John Dae wrapped Jean tightly against the thickness of his chest and pressed his tear-stained face, rough with a day's whiskers, against her own.

"I'm sorry," Jean whispered. "I'm so sorry."

"It's all right," he said, releasing his hold. "She knew. She knew you were just late."

She didn't understand, but whatever he needed to believe to get through this she would accept. She nodded and let him take her hands and squeeze them in the thick warmth of his own.

Marlene turned at the sound of their voices. "Jean, oh, Jean," she said wiping her tears. She reached for Jean's arm and pulled her to the side of the bed. "Look."

Jean shook her reluctance and looked at Lindy's face. There was no measure for her shock. Lindy's clear blue eyes were looking at the ceiling and moving slowly from side to side.

"She's waking up." Marlene's voice quivered with excitement. "It started with her hand—it began moving on the sheet near the side of the bed, here, where you always sit." She smiled and wiped the wetness from her cheeks. "I think she was looking for you, trying to find your hand."

"Oh my God," Jean whispered. She sat quickly in her usual chair and took Lindy's hand. "I'm here, Lindy. It's Ms. Carson. I was late, but I'm here now." The blue eyes moved in the direction of Jean's voice but did not seem to focus. "Can she hear me?"

The nurse had returned and positioned herself at the opposite side of the bed. "You can hear us, can't you, sweetie? Can you squeeze my hand for me?"

All eyes centered on the nurse's hand, watching for the barely noticeable delayed response.

"That's my girl, Lindy. Can you squeeze it harder?" Another delayed response. "Good, good. Can you squeeze Ms. Carson's hand with your other hand?"

Jean squeezed lightly and waited. "Yes, Lindy," she said excitedly. "Yes, I felt it."

"She's on her way back," the nurse explained. "She's on the light edge of the coma, but she's almost home. The doctor wants to see her in a few minutes. Why don't you all go have coffee, and I'll send him down to talk with you when he's through here."

The family waiting room stirred with questions and thankful celebration. Relief showed in their smiles, their eyes were dry now and sparkled with hope.

"How long will it take?"

"Will she be normal right away?"

"Will she remember everything?"

Marlene could not wait another minute to contact her other children. There was no need for James to skip classes again tomorrow, no need for Brandon to miss work, no need for Cathy to pack up two kids and think about another plane trip. They would be relieved on every count.

John engaged Shayna in a discussion about the possibility and improbability of legal action against whoever was responsible for what had happened to his daughter.

Jean listened and watched Shayna. She looked straight at her, and the pleasure that it brought was barely manageable. The feeling made her giddy and warm with anticipation. This was the woman she loved—caring, forgiving, patient—and very attractive.

She liked the tilt of her head as she listened, and the wide set of her shoulders, the way she used her hands to shape certain words as she spoke. So many things about this woman that pinked Jean's cheeks and quickened her heart. And freedom of mind, where all other thought is blotted out by the excitement of sexual desire, hadn't been there for some time. Tonight the only thing that would keep her from satisfying that desire would be setback news from the doctor.

Minutes later, the doctor arrived in the waiting room. "This is the kind of energy I love to feel when I come into the room," he said. "It's been a long time in coming, and I know you have lots of questions, so I'll get right to it for you." He pulled up an empty chair and closed the circle. "Things are looking a whole lot better. As the nurse explained, Lindy is still on the edge of a light coma, but she seems to be gaining steadily. It wouldn't be unusual, however, for her to plateau at some stage and seem to not be progressing. It's something we can't predict. I am going to have the neurologist see her tomorrow and give me his best assessment of her progress. Then I'll be able to give you better answers as to how quickly we might expect her to return to normal both physically and mentally."

John, leaning forward in his chair. "Will her memory be affected?"

"Short-term memory, yes, but long-term memory is something we can't be sure of. But the fact that she seems to recognize names is a very good sign."

"What keeps her from just waking up?" Marlene asked.

"Again, there's a lot we don't know. We know that the drug retards—no, let me use a better word here—impedes the brain's ability to send voluntary impulses. And it also does to the mind what alcohol does to an alcoholic when they black out; there is no memory at all of what happened. Combine the drug with alcohol and you can see why it's so effective for date rape. The body regains voluntary controls as the drug wears off and is eliminated from the body. But in the case of an overdose like Lindy suffered, the body regains control a little at a time over an extended period. We don't know how much of the drug she ingested, and so we have no gauge to measure if and when her responses will be normal again."

There were questions she wanted to ask, but Jean hesitated. It seemed more appropriate for the Daes to ask them. She would wait and ask only if they didn't.

"What is the chance that she will remember who gave her the drink?" Shayna asked.

The doctor shook his head. "Again, that's something we

179

can't predict. Probably remote, though," he replied, and pressed his lips tightly.

"We've avoided this question partly because, compared to life and death, it didn't—" John looked down in discomfort "—but it is important." He looked at the doctor. "Can you tell us if she was raped?"

"There was evidence of semen on her jeans and underwear, but we found no evidence of penetration."

There was an air of instant relief in the room as Marlene leaned into her husband's embrace.

The doctor continued. "Marlene, you indicated that you wanted to stay with Lindy tonight. I think that would be good, for your peace of mind. And, in case she does become more alert, it would be helpful for her to see a familiar face." He stood and leaned down to grasp Marlene's hand. "But remember, it may be a while yet. Sleep well everyone. I'll see you tomorrow."

Sleep well. Jean smiled to herself. Eventually, she would do just that.

Thirty-five

The envelope had remained in the same place on the coffee table for the past week. Unsorted junk mail, the Sunday newspaper, and the latest copy of Real Sports had aided Jean's avoidance. An odd assortment of mail retrieved from Jean's apartment had taken over the usual spot for case-study spreads, which would not have remained there long. Shayna attributed it to domestic sharing.

"Honey," she called, "are you through with the paper?" A cable advertisement went into the wastebasket, followed immediately by two unopened credit card applications, a drugstore flyer, and a mail-order catalogue. A full page of colorful pizza coupons was spared.

"Yes, I'm through with it," Jean replied as she entered the room. "Here, I'll take it to the recycle bin."

"While you're here, please open this letter."

Jean took the envelope with a sigh.

"You can't just ignore it."

"I didn't want to spoil the excitement of Lindy's improvement and being here with you. It's from the school-board. I know what it says."

Shayna maintained eye contact.

Jean relented and tore open the envelope. She read quickly and dropped the paper onto the table. " 'Your attendance is requested.' As I said, no surprises."

"When is the meeting?"

"Tomorrow night."

Shayna frowned. "When were you going to open it?"

"Tomorrow. "

Shayna retrieved the letter. "Did they give any specifics?"

She read aloud, "… will be addressing school policy and your personal and professional involvement regarding recent events surrounding student Lindy Dae."

"I knew it was coming." Jean sat down next to Shayna on the couch. "I've been crawling under his skin all year, and he's tired of the irritation. He'll justify his means, and he's not above exaggerating and manipulating the facts to make his case. If he can't make enough out of insubordination, he'll go after my sexuality."

"Then you have to deny it so that you can fight the insubordination. You'll have the legal support of both your local and state education associations. That's what you pay dues for."

"I never imagined needing them for anything except negotiating a new contract. There is another route he can take. He can continue until he makes my life so miserable at school that I'll leave voluntarily."

"Then you'll document everything that happens every day and present weekly logs to your union representative. You have the right to a hassle-free work environment."

"I have kept a log, but our union rep has been kind of weak in the past."

"Go up the line to your regional representative and demand protection. I'll be right beside you, advising you, advising them if need be. You won't have to do this alone."

"I have a new appreciation of what Katherine has had to go through. Unless you've experienced discrimination, you can't truly understand how painful it is."

Thirty-six

"Are you sure about this, Jean? I don't mind being there. I could sit in the back and you wouldn't have to worry about explaining who I am. But you would know that I'm there."

Shayna stopped the car in the partially filled staff lot. Jean took her hand before she could turn off the key.

"I'll be all right. You've given me good advice, and I know you'll be there when it's over. I have to do this by myself."

"I won't chance a kiss here," Shayna said with a gentle smile, "but you know I want to."

"Yes, I do, and I love you for it."

"If you need me, I'll be at the diner down the street. Call me when you're through. And remember, if anyone makes any accusations you tell them they'll have to speak with your attorney."

Jean nodded as she exited the car. "It shouldn't be too late; I'm third on the agenda." She made eye contact before shutting the door. "I'll be all right."

"I know you will. I love you."

She hadn't said it to ease Shayna's concerns or even to bolster her own confidence. It was true. She would be fine. She had arrived at the place where her anxiety needed the relief of confrontation, and she was ready to have it over. Ready to face what she once

183

thought she never could, with the strength of spirit that would survive what used to be her worst fear.

Tonight she welcomed the chance to step up to another level. She had made a difference where she was, developed her programs, fought for their continuance, and now she had the opportunity to step up to a bigger challenge. As she thought about it, she realized that she wouldn't be satisfied at status quo, knowing that if only she would take the risk and take the challenge maybe she could do much more.

Fate was a concept Jean had dismissed more than once, along with God's master plan. Both involved too much trust and too little control. Neither offered a guarantee that she would reach the goals she set for her life.

Lately, though, with her life taking turns that she hadn't expected, she was giving fate another look. She hated to call it fate, but that came close to answering what she couldn't explain. When the direction of her life reached an impasse and her energy ran to exhaustion attempting to push on, something changed the direction. Forced by exhaustion and frustration to stop, she had little choice but to watch and wait. And when she did, things began happening on their own. Obstacles disappeared, making way for her energy to surge full power down a new path. She could finally tuck her oar and ride the easy current. Why must we spend so much of our lives swimming upstream before we understand that we aren't salmon?

The room began to fill with more than the usual number of parents and teachers. It hadn't taken long for word to travel. Most monthly meetings dealt with mundane business decisions and drew little interest from the public. School-bond discussions, contract negotiations, program cuts, and complaints involving teachers or students—those were issues that could pack the room.

Jean smiled at supportive colleagues and familiar parents, wondered how much effect their presence would have, and avoided eye contact with Ellerton. Brian claimed the seat next to her.

"Hey, good lookin'," he greeted.

"What," Jean asked, looking at the leather contraption he dropped in her lap, "is this?"

"Your slingshot," he said, nodding toward the front of the room. "To face the Philistine."

Perfectly and typically irreverent. "Are you telling me how bad the odds are or how much faith you have in me?"

"Both."

Despite the embarrassing kinds of questions that she was about to face, she was glad that he was here. As for everyone else, she would try to block them out. Her answers could not be made for their benefit.

"What do you know about the two new board members?" she asked.

"They've stayed very quiet. One's a small business owner; the other's an insurance agent. Not ones to start a tidal wave."

The last of the board members took his seat at the semicircle of tables at the front of the room. The superintendent called the meeting to order with a cordial greeting, noted that all board members were present, and called for the first order of business. Approval of expenditures, acceptance of the treasurer's report, and conclusion of old business were all efficiently disposed of within an hour.

Chad Ellerton's report was the next order of business. He moved to the microphone. With each methodical step, Jean's pulse pounded louder in her ears. She tried deep, slow breaths to stop the sudden sense of nausea, but they started the acids bubbling up from her stomach. She swallowed the bitterness as Brian gave her hand a squeeze. She hated lying to him.

Within the next hour, she would know whether she'd be challenging a wrongful dismissal or preparing for a harassment case. The questions in her head muted Ellerton's voice. Could you have handled the situation differently? Would you in the future? Did you advise or influence this student's sexuality? Are the rumors of your own sexuality true? She took another deep breath. Submit and deny, she reminded herself. It will be over soon.

One cup of coffee and a once-over review of a new case was all the time Shayna could justify in the diner. The least she could do was sip takeout and wait in the parking lot so that Jean wouldn't have to wait a minute more than necessary.

She made sporadic attempts to speak notes into a tape recorder, but found it difficult to concentrate. Visions of Jean standing alone before the board, before her colleagues, returned each time. And each time she could sense her apprehension, feel the heat of her embarrassment, and hear the echo of the questions. She saw Jean's face, flushed and serious, and her eyes wide and waiting. By now, Jean would have torn the freshly healed skin from around her fingernails, leaving them raw and painful once again. And there was nothing Shayna could do to make things easier for her.

She sighed and whispered into the dark interior of the car. "I love you, baby. It'll be over soon." *And when it is I'll take you home and hold you close and show you how much I love you.*

The sound of the phone made her jump. She reached for her own, but on the second ring she realized that it was Jean's phone, still in her bag on the floor. *My poor love, you never forget your bag.* Shayna retrieved it quickly.

"Hello … No, may I take a message for her? Yes. Yes, Marlene, this is Shayna." *Please, Marlene, only good news tonight.* "Oh, that is good news … No, I didn't expect that either … Absolutely. Have John call me tomorrow … I certainly will tell her. She'll appreciate your calling. Good night, Marlene."

Armed now with more than supportive arms to comfort her, Shayna watched anxiously for Jean as people began emerging from the school entrance. Jean was, as expected, among the first to leave. With careful footing she made her way to the car by following large boot prints through the snow-bank. She slid into the front seat, dropped her head against the headrest, closed her eyes, and let out a long breath.

Shayna took her hand and spared her any more questions. There would be time enough later. Right now, she needed to lift the pale from her lover's cheeks. "I'll tell you something good," she said with a squeeze of Jean's hand. "Jay Markus walked into the police station with his mother and told it all. Your instinct about him was right. He stopped Jason Weeks from raping her and got Lindy to the parking lot."

No movement from Jean. She stared straight ahead with no change of expression. "There was a hero inside."

Yes there was, a heroine, a beautiful heroine, Shayna thought, looking at the woman she loved. She turned the key and started for home.

Suddenly, Jean turned. "There were letters I didn't know about. You think you know people …"

"Letters? Complaints or—"

"And teachers and Lindy's counselor asked to speak," Jean continued.

Shayna pulled to the curb and gave her her full attention. There was still a look of stunned surprise in Jean's eyes. "The board has asked me to chair a committee to formulate district guidelines to deal with sexual harassment."

"Oh yes," Shayna exclaimed, "and me this time with little faith. My God, baby, why aren't you ecstatic?"

"I don't remember if I said yes."

Marianne K. Martin

Marianne K. Martin is one of the top selling lesbian romance authors in the country and her books have gained a wide international readership. Her highly successful novels include the Lambda Literary Award finalists *Under the Witness Tree*, *Mirrors*, and *For Now, For Always*. Marianne is also one of the founding partners here at Bywater Books. Her duties at Bywater include acquisitions, managing the Bywater Prize for Fiction, and working with Bywater's new writers.

Bywater Books

UNDER THE WITNESS TREE
Marianne K. Martin

"*Under the Witness Tree* is a multi-dimensional love story woven with rich themes of family and the search for roots. This is a novel of discovery that reaches into the deeply personal and well beyond—into our community and its emerging history. Marianne Martin achieves new heights with this lovingly researched and intelligent novel."

—*Katherine V. Forrest*

An aunt she didn't know existed leaves Dhari Weston with a plantation she knows she doesn't want.

Dhari's life is complicated enough without an antebellum albatross around her neck. Complicated enough without the beautiful Erin Hughes and her passion for historical houses, without Nessie Tinker, whose family breathed the smoke of General Sherman's march and who knows the secrets hidden in the ancient walls—secrets that could pull Dhari into their sway and into Erin's arms.

But Dhari's complicated life already includes a girlfriend she wants to commit to, a family who needs her to calm the chaos of her mother's turbulent moods and a job that takes the rest of her time.

The last thing she needs are Civil War secrets that won't lie easy and a woman with secrets of her own ...

Paperback Original ◆ ISBN 1-932859-00-4 ◆ $12.95

Available at your local bookstore
or call 734-662-8815
or order online at www.bywaterbooks.com

Bywater Books

LAST CHANCE AT THE LOST AND FOUND

Marcia Finical

In 1972 Bunny LaRue was young and beautiful. Days in the sun on the beach at Malibu and nights in the bars with the girls. Sex, drugs, and fun were everywhere and Bunny embraced it all.

After a photographer sees her on the beach Bunny finds herself making big money modeling for a lingerie catalog. Then she falls in love and life seems to be giving her everything she has ever wanted—until the day she loses it all.

As the years slip by life doesn't stay easy and Bunny must find the strength to confront her past and create a new future …

Last Chance at the Lost and Found is the compelling story of one woman's journey through twenty-five years of living as a lesbian and her determination to find love and happiness.

Last Chance at the Lost and Found is the winner of the first annual Bywater Prize for Fiction.

Paperback Original ◆ ISBN 978-1-932859-28-7 ◆ $13.95

Available at your local bookstore
or call 734-662-8815
or order online at www.bywaterbooks.com

Bywater Books

VERGE

Z Egloff

"*Verge* is powerful, quirky, and fresh."
—Alison Bechdel, author of *Fun Home*,
Time Magazine's Best Book of 2006

Claire has three goals: to stay sober, to stay away from sex, and to get into film school. So far she's blown two of the three and her drunken affair with her professor's wife means she might just have blown the third. Stuck without the camera she needs to complete her course work, she turns to Sister Hilary at the community center for help. Sister Hilary has a camera to lend, but the price is recruiting Claire as a reluctant volunteer. The only trouble is, Claire's more attracted to Sister Hilary than to helping out.

Claire ought to know there's no future with a nun, but can't this two-timing, twelve-stepping, twenty-something film freak get a chance at happiness?

Verge is the winner of the fourth annual
Bywater Prize for Fiction.

Paperback Original ◆ ISBN 978-1-932859-68-3 ◆ $14.95

Available at your local bookstore
or call 734-662-8815
or order online at www.bywaterbooks.com

Bywater Books represents the coming of age of lesbian fiction. We're committed to bringing the best of contemporary lesbian writing to a discerning readership. Our editorial team is dedicated to finding and developing outstanding voices who deliver stories you won't want to put down. That's why we sponsor the annual Bywater Prize. We love good books, just like you do.

For more information about Bywater Books and the annual Bywater Prize for Fiction, please visit our website.

www.bywaterbooks.com